THE FIRE
THAT BURNS

THE FIRE THAT BURNS

MARK TRYON

CUTTING EDGE

ISBN-13: 978-1-952138-68-3

Published by
Cutting Edge Books
PO Box 8212
Calabasas, CA 91372
www.cuttingedgebooks.com

BOOK ONE—THE FIRE

CHAPTER ONE

J aney Hamsun picked her way through the sun-spattered pine woods, leaving road and trail behind, having decided in a fit of high spirits to strike out cross-country for the little river.

Janey enjoyed the feeling of being completely alone—of being cut off from all other people—deep in a virtual wilderness. There was a sense of relief in the experience. Not that she did not enjoy the continual parties and houseguests at her mother's big lodge on the lake shore. But there *were* times when the laughter and music and the continual clinking of ice in tall glasses became an unbearable din in her ears. At such times she would go off by herself, staying away whole days at a time.

No one missed her particularly. Her mother and her mother's friends were preoccupied with their own pastimes.

She whistled gaily as she stepped gingerly over fallen logs and skirted little clumps of dense underbrush. Janey was happy. There was something about the woods, about the crazy-quilt pattern of the sun-spots, about the little rustling sounds of the trees, about the wildnerness-silence, broken now and again by the fluting of a bird or the tiny laughter of the chipmunks. Something that fitted her mood, something that made her feel light and gay.

Eventually she broke from the cover of the trees out onto the little strip of sandy shore, which she had never seen before, but which somehow seemed familiar. She looked about, her face radiant with an inner exultation.

What on earth was wrong with her? She could not remember ever having felt like this before. She threw her little blonde head back and laughed out loud. What a feeling! What a wonderful feeling!

Janey threw herself on the warm sand and stretched her slender limbs. A small golden girl in the golden sand, her blonde hair falling softly on her shoulders, her trim body sleek and delicate and youthful.

She drank in the sylvan scene about her. At the spot where she was lying, the little river which served as the inlet for the large lake on the shore of which her mother's elaborate lodge was situated broadened out into a deep—apparently tranquil—pool, clear and transparent as crystal. The lacelike willows leaned over the water in gentle intimacy, and beyond the willows stood the enormous Technicolored yellow-pines, their gaudy orange bark in brilliant contrast to the deep green of their long, slender needles.

A quick sound from the pool made Janey sit up abruptly. Smiling, she watched the ever-widening circle where the rainbow trout had leaped, its gaping mouth grasping for the elusive fly. The water, the trout, the peacefulness and seclusion of the scene gave her an idea, and slyly, like a girl at the jampot, she stood up. Her eyes slid slowly about her, making a complete circle, reassuring her that she was indeed alone…alone as she could ever be with the trees and the wind and the little animals.

Satisfied, she went to the edge of the pool and knelt down. She ran her hand through the water, reveling in its cool cleanness. Suddenly she stood up and her hands went to her right side, the fingers closing over the zipper-lock.

For a brief moment she stood like that, her mind not quite made up after all. What a strange feeling was in her. What a wild feeling of abandonment. She stood there, her legs pressed tightly together under the cover of her skirt, her heart beating wildly. Suddenly she felt the loneliness. It came upon her as a surprising wave of despair. She looked about her, as if expecting someone, her arms yearning, her fingers curling on the zipper-lock as if they hungered to touch and grasp. As if they wanted to violate. Violate? The word rang strangely in her head. Violate what?

Then the feeling of despair left her and the loneliness went away and was replaced by a kind of breathless expectation. With a swift jerk she ripped the zipper open. She pulled the bright yellow dress over her head. The yellow nylon slip followed.

Janey had a funny little quirk. She loved color, all color except white. To her, white was dull and uninteresting. Her mother, however, felt very strongly on the subject of white underwear for young ladies. "There is something clean and fresh about it," she would say, "there's something decent and modest about it."

But Janey hated white. So when her mother bought her white underthings Janey would get dye in all sorts of outrageous colors and change them. Purple, green, yellow, blue—she even fixed herself a scarlet set once. But after she had done it she had never had the nerve to wear it. It was as if she were afraid that someone would see it under her frock and slip. She *was* afraid that someone would see it, and at the same time she kind of *wanted* someone to see it.

Now she stood revealed on the shore of the little pool in a completely transparent net brassiere and a pair of brief opened-legged satin panties, both dyed a soft apple-green. Had anyone been there to see her, it would have been a sight he would never have forgotten. Her golden hair and fair skin were displayed to their very best advantage by the soft green of the panties and brassiere. Janey was a beautiful girl. Breathtakingly beautiful.

After a small moment of slightly shamed hesitation, she reached both hands behind her back and unsnapped the brassiere. She removed it and dropped it on the ground. The small, young cups of her breasts stood free and proud from her chest, the little pink rosebuds on them crinkling slightly in the cooling breeze.

Janey stretched and ran her hands down over her breasts in a sudden, unexpectedly lascivious gesture. Her hands continued their downward journey, gliding over her waist, her fingers entangling themselves in the elastic of the panties and then continuing downward until they were peeled from her hips and had fallen in a small heap about her feet. She stepped free of them and stood naked, the curves of her hips shining with a velvet sheen in the afternoon sun.

She had a sudden impulse to hug her arms about herself, to hid, to cover up her shamelessness. But then she reminded herself that she was entirely alone, and laughingly she ran to the edge of the pool. On the very brink she stopped, naked and gleaming and unbelievably lovely. Her eyes regarded her own image in the quiet water and the image pleased her beyond description. Shuddering deliciously, she ran the tips of her fingers ever so delicately over her breasts. She felt the rosy points harden and with a quick, sudden movement she stopped and flung herself into the beckoning stream.

The cold water assaulted her warm skin and she came to the surface gasping and laughing and crying out with the sudden cold-pain. Then she struck out from shore, her arms flashing and her white back barely showing beneath the surface.

She was swimming straight out toward the center of the pool when she first felt the unexpected current, the tugging undertow, backed and propelled by all the power of the little river. Frightened, she turned back toward her starting point, but the current was stronger than she. She struggled frantically against it, but it pulled her along with it nevertheless, slowly, inexorably sucking her down into its gaping, seething maw, hidden so treacherously beneath the tranquil, smiling surface of the apparently harmless pool.

Janey tried to scream, but her mouth filled with water. Her body fought with the dreadful strength of deadly terror, but the waters drew her ever farther down.

At last the living, carnivorous river flung her playfully from its whirlpool mouth and for a brief instant her small white body gleamed wetly in the sun. Then it sucked her back into its gaping death and she disappeared from the surface, the pale blonde hair following her down like floating silver strands, becoming shorter and shorter until they too disappeared and only the calmness of the little pool remained, peaceful and sylvan and inviting.

Pat Mulroney carefully fitted the yellow filter into the lens-shade and the lens-shade onto the lens of his Speed-Graphic. Then, climbing over the side of the boat in his rolled-up khaki pants, he stepped into the shallow water. He edged himself as close to the lake shore as he could and squatted down, the camera held just barely above the water surface.

The overhanging willow made a beautiful foreground frame for the distant giant tamaracks whose delicate needle-pattern looked like Brussels lace against the cotton clouds and the cobalt sky.

He straightened up and took his meter-reading carefully, aware that the reflection from the lake could fool the photoelectric cell badly. The meter read 1/100th of a second at F16 and this seemed reasonable to him. He set the time and aperture adjustments carefully and laid out his composition on the ground glass. Satisfied, he slipped the film holder into place, cocked his shutter, pulled the slide, shot the picture—the camera glued against his face—replaced the slide, and straightened up with a deep sigh of relief.

That was that! The last one. Now it was just a matter of do or die.

He climbed back into the little rented boat, laid the camera carefully on the seat with his other equipment, lifted the cord of the light-meter from around his neck and tucked the meter into the gadget bag. He zipped up the bag and sat down in the back of the boat with a sense of satisfaction and completion.

He picked up one of the oars and started lazily paddling along the shore, steeped in self-contemplation. Pat Mulroney.

Recently of Marquis College, now graduated and launched into the wide, wide world to flounder and struggle to keep his head above the waters of the giant river of success that would carry him either to the rocks of failure or to the ocean of success.

He grinned wryly at himself. Brother, *there* was a bit of deathless prose.

A cloud of worry passed over his face. Deathless prose or no deathless prose, this last batch of pictures had better be the ones. They had *better* be the ones, all right, and no funny fooling. If they weren't, Mrs. Mulroney's little boy had better abandon the present course of action and find another way to keep body and soul together. All his eggs were in this one basket. Five hundred dollars worth of eggs. Five hundred dollars laboriously saved from the thousand odd jobs of four years of college. A little lawnmowing here, a little dishwashing there, a little tutoring here, a little camp-counseling there, a little of this, a little of that. Five hundred smackers! Three hundred for equipment and two hundred for a month of trying. After that... well, if nothing materialized, if no enthusiastic offers poured in from *Natural History Magazine* or *National Geographic* or *Outdoor Life*—okay, the handwriting would be on the wall. But meanwhile, why worry?

He looked about with pleasure. Everywhere, on every hand, were pictures. He could not have chosen a better place to try to prove his value in the field. Yes, he had prepared this whole campaign with care. Unlike so many college seniors, he had chosen a profession and had done everything he could to master that profession. Now he only hoped that the profession would pay him back in kind. Oh, well. Time would tell.

His boat nosed against the bank and gently wedged itself against a waterlogged stump. There it stuck and he let it stay while he watched the swiftly moving water of the river. On the opposite shore two gleaming muskrats emerged from the bushes, playing, teasing each other, nipping at each other's oily fur with tiny teeth, rolling on the ground in tight embrace. Pat watched them and smiled. Boy, were they lucky!

Then he saw the trap that some fur-hungry hunter had set and he saw the little animals unsuspectingly moving closer and closer in their play. He started to push his boat from the shore to cross over and spring the trap and save the gay little creatures. Then the thought struck him—the hunter has a profession, too, doesn't he? He is not a heedless killer. He sells fur. Well, how do you get fur?

Dog eat dog. He arrested himself in mid-impulse and just then he heard the sickening sound of the trap and the little scream. He watched in horror as one of the muskrats continued playing with the trapped one, believing its convulsions and whimpering to be part of the play. His eyes turned away as the feeble sounds grew feebler, and when he looked again the little glistening body was lying limply at the water's edge, the chain of the trap drawn out to its fullest extent. The other muskrat was gone.

A deep depression settled on him, but even at the same moment he knew that there was a touching human-interest story in the little body and the mute, heroic stretch of the chain that showed how the courageous animal had tried to drag itself away from the mysterious enemy with the iron jaws. It would make a good shot if he could maneuver in for a close-up. Only that would necessitate a bit of wading. Aware that the water might be much deeper than it looked, even at the shore, he stripped to his skin.

He was getting his equipment together when he heard the strangled cry and saw the sudden flash of the white body in the sucking current of the river. Quickly he put down his camera and started along the stream where it shimmered and glared with the reflected light from the sun. He thought he must have had an hallucination, but then he saw the white body again, below the surface now, struggling spasmodically against the rushing current. Without a second thought he plunged into the treacher-ous water and started frantically swimming toward it.

The water had looked comparatively tame to him, and he was unpleasantly surprised at the fury of the torrential below-surface current when he hit it. He almost went down. Frantically he fought its power in horror that he might be too late. The white figure had disappeared and he ducked his head below the surface. He saw it clearly then. The slim, nude body of a young woman, quietly drifting and bumping along the bottom of the river.

He dove straight down, but the current carried him below her in a violent, down-dragging tug. He struggled back up and tried again. This time he barely managed to get hold of the girl's long free-floating hair. He twisted his fingers in it, put his feet against the stony bottom and pushed with all his might. He fairly flew to the surface, dragging the girl behind him.

The current had carried them out into the lake and they broke clear where the undertow had all but dissipated itself. Pat trod water and turned to get a better look at the girl, but just as he turned she flung her arms violently apart and started strug-gling insanely as though the current still had her in its grip. They almost went down together, but he maintained a desperate hold on her hair, pulling her suddenly against him. They were clutched in a tight, struggling, slithering embrace. Even in the struggle, with the deep, cold water all about them, Pat felt the effect of the slight, naked body which writhed against him. The small breasts were crushed against his chest and he felt their taut points bor-ing into his ribs. Her legs twined around his, her heels kicking ineffectually against his calves. The little face, just barely above the surface, was twisted into a horrible grimace with a gaping, gasping mouth and staring eyes.

The girl fought like a madwoman. The more she fought the more their mutual danger increased. He finally managed to twist her about so that her back was against him. He felt the wet soft-ness of her hips as he wrapped his right arm about her chest. He got a good grip on her struggling form, and with his left arm he struck out for the boat where it still lay in the mouth of the river.

After a short while she lay still and did not fight him any longer. Her lungs were heaving for air and her throat rattled with great, heaving coughs. As their feet touched bottom close to the boat, he lifted her up and carried her the rest of the way in both arms, her long blonde hair hanging down his side, her eyes closed, her breasts pushed together in such a way that they looked larger than they actually were. He raised her gently over the side and lowered her into the bottom of the boat. Then he reached for the large black camera-cloth and covered her with it, but not until he had seen how lovely she was—how slim and golden and utterly desirable. He did not remember his own nudity until he noticed her quick glance between gasping breaths and the embarrassed way in which she averted her eyes.

Thank God she didn't blush, he thought. He turned his back on her and climbed lightly into the boat. He reached for his trousers and pulled them on over the wetness of his body. Then he sank down on the stern seat and extracted two cigarets from the package that lay there. He lit both and held one out to her.

She shook her head. "Let me catch my breath first."

He threw her cigaret overboard and took a deep drag of his own. They remained like that for a long time, he sitting in the stern, she lying exhaustedly in the bottom, their eyes on each other.

Finally she looked down at herself. "I look like a body," she said a little breathlessly.

"You *are* quite a body." He smiled, but wished he had not said it when he noticed the embarrassment mounting in her eyes. "I'm sorry," he continued contritely, "this is no time to make a stupid joke. You came about as close to being killed as you ever will, I guess."

She nodded and her face took on a faraway look that startled him. It put a mask of age across her features, as if she were looking into a world where he could not follow her. Finally she looked up at him. "Could I have that cigaret now?" she asked, and he found her voice soft and melodious, now that the harshness was gone from her throat.

He nodded and picked up the pack. She started to sit up as he extracted the cigaret from the crumpled wrapper. The black flannel slid from her shoulders and she clutched it desperately about her chest and her forearm.

They looked at each other and laughed. He stuck the cigaret in her mouth and lit it. After a couple of deep puffs she asked, "You don't happen to have anything I could put on, do you? Perhaps we could get to know each other a little better if I didn't have to hang on to this postage stamp of a piece of material quite so desperately."

He looked away. He had something she could wear all right, but he felt like a fool offering it to her. "Well...." He hesitated. "Well, yes, if you don't mind—"

"Honest, I don't mind anything except this foolish position I am in."

"Well, look, you could put on my shirt and ... and my shorts. At least they would cover you," he added hastily.

She laughed a wonderful clear, pealing laughter. "Give 'em to me," she gasped, as the wracking cough returned. She took the shirt and shorts from him. "Turn your back," she said. Then she laughed and had to stop for breath again before she could continue. "Although that may be a needless formality after our recent intimacy."

He sat looking out over the water, watching the swallows swooping low for their evening bath, seeing a white-collared loon floating majestically on the surface, seeing the clouds and the sky, but actually seeing nothing because he heard the sounds of her dressing behind him and felt the rocking of the boat as she shifted her weight and his inner eye saw something entirely different from the swallows and the loon and the clouds and the sky.

"You can turn around now." He heard the giggle in her voice and swung about and laughed out loud when he saw the spectacle she presented. She had put on his shorts and shirt, the tail of which hung almost to her knees, hiding all but a fleeting glimpse of the shorts. She had taken his comb and run it through her long, wet hair so that it hung like a gold curtain surrounding her little face. She was unbelievably beautiful, he thought, and unbelievably radiant and amusing. Her blue eyes twinkled merrily and her mouth smiled at him, showing white even teeth between lips that were red even though they did not have a touch of lipstick on them. There was no trace of embarrassment about her, although she certainly must have known that she was not the most fashionable young lady he had ever seen, decked out as she was in that outlandish costume.

She sat down on the seat in the center of the boat, her elbows on her knees. "Well," she said. "That's that."

"Isn't that a fact," he ventured and then, strangely, he did not know what to say. It was as if this merry girl had robbed him of the power of speech. As if she had glued his tongue to the roof of his mouth. He swallowed painfully and saw that she was amused at his discomfiture.

"Oh, come now," she giggled. "We know each other too well to be embarrassed."

"*You* were embarrassed," he accused.

"Isn't that a fact," she mimicked, a little wryly. "But then, it isn't every day I go buck swimming with a strange man."

"You sure scared me."

"I was a little scared myself." She grew suddenly serious. "Thank you," she said. "Thank you for saving my life." She was quiet for a moment. Then, "My name is Jane Hamsun. I live here during the summer with my mother."

He reached out an awkward hand. "I'm Pat Mulroney," he said. "I've lived here this past month—with my camera."

She smiled. "With your camera?" She pressed his hand warmly.

"Yes. I'm a photographer."

"I'd love to see some of your pictures sometime."

"I'd ... I'd be happy to show them to you." There was a long pause. Dammit anyway! What do you say to a girl you have just saved from drowning?

"Where are you staying?" she asked.

"Oh, I stay over on the other side of the lake."

"You mean at the Lemmings'?"

"Yes. In one of the cabins."

"Well then, you must be going to the square dance tonight, aren't you?"

"No. No, I wasn't figuring to."

"I'm so sorry. I thought maybe I might see you there."

"You will. You certainly will," he said hastily.

She looked at him, puzzled. "I thought you said you weren't going."

"Oh, that was last week," he stammered like a fool. "I thought you meant last week."

She looked at him as though he were demented. Then she stood up. "I know this sounds crazy," she said, "but could I give you back your shorts and shirt when I see you tonight?"

"Sure," he said. "Why, sure. Keep them, if you want to," he added, realizing miserably as he said it that he was rapidly turning himself into a driveling idiot.

"I've got some pants of my own," she giggled and jumped from the boat to the shore. "Thank you again," she said, turning. "I want you to get to know my mother tonight. She'll want to meet my gallant rescuer." She started off. Then she turned. "Don't tell her how I was dressed," she added, amusement crinkling her face.

"Oh, I wouldn't dream of it," he said and jumped to the shore. "Can't I take you back to wherever you're going?"

"No! No, thank you. I'll manage all right." She ran off through the woods, her laughter dying away as she disappeared.

Like a complete idiot Pat stood staring after her, his mouth hanging open. Suddenly he turned and made a wild leap for the boat. He was in a hurry. He had to get back to shave and get dressed for the dance.

His wild leap missed the boat and with a huge splash he fell into the water where he lay, staring at the sky but seeing nothing, listening to the river but hearing nothing…

… only her, only her, only her!

CHAPTER TWO

The mirror reflected her image perfectly. Janey twisted and turned in front of it. She adjusted the lights at either side and stepped back, the better to see herself.

She heard the laughter from downstairs where her mother and that French actor were drinking together.

"Cinderella," she said aloud, "they don't even know you exist." Her eyes caressed her image again, running the full length of the pale mauve evening gown, over the small heart-shaped face, the long golden hair, the red, red lips. She put her hands on herself and was immensely pleased. She blew a kiss at herself and backed away from the mirror even farther, twirling the skirt of the gown, swinging her body in a gay imaginary dance.

She sobered suddenly. *What is the matter with me these days?* She turned out the lights and opened the door and started downstairs.

Her mother regarded her with amazement over the edge of her glass. "Good grief, honey!" she ejaculated.

Jacques Fribeaux jumped to his feet from where he had been sitting on the raised stone hearth. "Janey!" he cried and came toward her, one hand extended. "*Mon dieu,* what an entrance!"

"Monsieur Fribeaux." Janey swept into a deep curtsy as she reached the floor of the living room. "How about a drink for me?"

"One," her mother said. "Only one!"

Fribeaux turned toward Nell Hamsun, his voice strangely angry. "Mademoiselle is no child, my dear. It would be well if you could remember that."

Nell Hamsun smiled good-naturedly. "All right, all right, Jacques. I'm sorry. My motherly instinct and all that."

Fribeaux turned back to Janey. "May I escort mademoiselle to the well of poison?" he asked and extended his arm.

"Avec plaisir," she answered in her best school-girl French. Then she laughed. "Jacques, for goodness' sake, can't we speak English or some other language I know, like Sanskrit, so that I can hold up my end of the conversation?"

"With pleasure, my Janey." He laughed and as they started toward the bar at the lower end of the huge, semi-rustic, semi-modernistic living room, he asked, "What'll it be? How's that? Is that good American? *Oui? Non?*"

"Oui," said Janey. "Very fine, average, wholesome American. I'll have a Scotch-on-the-rocks."

"Janey!"

"A little won't hurt me, mother."

"But it's such a vulgar drink."

Fribeaux looked at Nell Hamsun slyly. "What's yours, my dear?" he asked.

"Another of the same."

"Scotch straight," said Fribeaux, smiling at Janey. "Tsk, tsk, tsk. Like mother, like child. That is also good American, *non?*"

"Not very grammatical, but good American, you fugitive from the Foreign Legion." Janey laughed.

Fribeaux made the drinks, patiently going through the motions of carefully measuring the liquor from a jigger.

"Are you going to the square dance in that dress?" Nell asked.

"Why not?"

"Isn't it a little … eh, pretentious?"

"Pretentious? Why?"

"Well, I mean … this is a country square-dance, isn't it?"

"To us, maybe, yes."

"What do you mean, to us?"

"I mean it's strictly country-bumpkin and all that to us. But to the local people it is dead serious. I mean … you meet young men there and all … I mean, well, you want to look your best."

Nell stood up. She was a strikingly beautiful woman, but unlike Janey she was dark and buxom and powerful-looking. Exotic. Somehow, she looked vaguely Latin-American. There was not a trace of gray in her hair, although Janey knew her to admit to fifty years. "What, exactly, do you mean by *meeting young men?*"

Janey accepted her drink from Fribeaux. She walked toward Nell, meeting her in the middle of the floor. "I mean exactly that, mother," she said.

"Who?"

"I almost drowned this afternoon," Janey said casually.

Nell said, "What's that got to do with it?" Then the full impact penetrated and she looked horrified. "You almost *what?*"

"I almost drowned this afternoon." Janey was loving her moment. It was so rarely that she had her mother's full attention. She wanted to drag it out and drag it out.

"Drowned?" cried Nell. She grasped Janey's shoulders with her powerful hands. "Where? How?"

"I went swimming in the inlet."

"Yes?"

"There's an awful undertow. I didn't know about it." Janey giggled, enjoying herself thoroughly. "I went swimming in the raw and the current caught me."

"And somebody? Some *man* … saved you?"

"That's right."

"You were naked?"

"I guess you could call it that." Janey sauntered toward the fireplace.

"Janey!" Nell turned toward Fribeaux and found him grinning delightedly. With evident disgust she took her drink from his hand and crossed the seemingly endless floor to Janey.

"What *is* this all about?" She asked in that patient voice which Janey had learned to dread.

"It's nothing very much, mother. I went swimming in the inlet—"

"Nude?"

"Yes, mother."

"How could you do such a thing?"

"Mother, I almost drowned—don't you *care?*"

"Of course I care, but why nude?"

"I was all alone."

"All right, so you were alone. Now go on with your story."

"All right. I went swimming and got caught in the undertow of the river, that's all. It just sucked me down and I almost drowned."

"Why, that's awful, Janey. Awful!" Nell put an arm around her. "If I had lost you, I … why, I …" The tone of her voice changed subtly. "Who is this man who saved you?"

"He's a photographer."

"What's his name?"

"Why, I … Pat, he said. I don't know what his last name is."

"You don't *know?*"

"Mother, it was not exactly a time for cool, calm nerves."

"But didn't he tell you?"

"Of course he did. I just didn't pay any attention."

"Well, of all the …" Nell swung away.

"Mother, mother, there's nothing to get angry about. It was just an accident."

"*Just* an accident? Here you are, nude and drowning and some … some stray man hauls your naked body out of the water."

Janey giggled. "*He* was naked, too."

"He was *what?*"

The scene was broken in the middle by the uproarious laughter of Jacques Fribeaux. "Oh, *mon dieu,*" he gasped. "This poor old broken-down actor should have been there. What a scene!"

Janey turned boldly to her mother. "You go swimming in the nude yourself!"

Fribeaux exploded into uncontrollable laughter. "Thees," he cried, reverting to the accent which he had long ago shed, "thees ees ze funneeest theeng I have heard in yeeeers!"

Nell turned toward him menacingly. "You—" she cried in her worst fishmonger's tones. *"You shut up!"* Then she returned to Janey, an entirely new Nell Hamsun. "I'm sorry, honey," she said, the tones of her voice velvety soft, "I just got excited over what happened to you today without even realizing that you were in danger. Let's drink our drinks and go to the dance. We can talk about this later. Naturally I want to meet the young man. Please forgive me for getting excited. Of course, I go swimming myself in the nude sometimes. It *is* awfully pleasant, isn't it? Let's drink our drinks." She turned animatedly to Fribeaux. "To say the least, I *need* mine. Wouldn't you say I was entitled to it, Jacques? I almost lost a daughter today."

Janey regarded her mother as she joined the French actor by the bar. What was there about Nell that made Janey feel so ... so *strange* ... as if she couldn't trust her. Nell was her mother, wasn't she? Then why was it always this way?

Janey did not know her father, but somehow she knew that he must have been a wonderful man. Not because of anything her mother ever said. "I'm on my own," Nell would say. "I owe nothing to anybody and I am doing well. Very well, indeed," she would conclude, looking with satisfaction at the rustic richness of their mountain lodge, or with a kind of deep triumph at their town house in New York.

For that matter, other than the knowledge that it was *not* Hamsun, Janey did not even know the *name* of her father. Her mother had never mentioned it and Nell Hamsun was not the kind of woman you asked questions of easily. Nell had always managed to make any question about Janey's father seem unreasonable. So the time had come when Janey had stopped asking questions, although she had not given up thinking about him.

She looked about the luxurious room, which contained objects of furniture and art which would not have been found in the mountain lodge of a man. She wondered as she had always wondered where her mother got her money from. Then her glance slid to Jacques Fribeaux and the thought went through her head that her mother made her living off men. But she turned her mind away from the idea. No girl wants to think that of her mother, no matter how much her mother seems to be eternally—and with everlasting variety—successful with the men.

Her eyes strayed to the clock by the hall door. "Hey," she cried, "it's time! We're already an hour late."

"Ho!" Fribeaux cried. "Let us go and see the quaint native customs of these untamed American people!"

"Quaint isn't the word," said Nell dryly.

"Oh, mother, I think it's awfully exciting," cried Janey.

"I know you do," her mother answered.

Fribeaux looked at Janey and at her mother; then he said gently, "Where I come from, the country people dance, too. They are wonderful dancers. Every one of them. It is as if they suck the very sap of life and the strength of their dancing feet with their mother's milk. I think it is good that the urge to dance is in all people, don't you?"

"Oh, sure," Nell said.

Pat Mulroney entered the hall, dank with the smells of pine pitch and heady sweat, and sat down on the bench next to the door. The band struck up a tune and within five minutes he found himself in the thick of it, swinging a buxom, bemuscled maiden through the impossibly strenuous footwork of what is certainly the most athletic dance in the northern hemisphere.

As he danced, Pat thought sourly of the picture story he had done on the Lemmings and on their Saturday night dances.

The trappers and the ranchers and the Forest Service people had been intensely interested in him and his equipment. They had squealed with glee every time his flash equipment went off. They had invited him out to their trucks for a drink of "good ol' 'merican whiskey," until he had happily told everyone they would probably appear in *Life* before the summer was over. It had given them food for conversation for several weeks afterwards and he had become something of a hero among them. Now he thought of the thick envelope with returned pictures and the brief, friendly letter from the picture editor of the national magazine, explaining that he found the pictures excellent, but that unfortunately such a story was too commonplace to make good feature material. He had not had the nerve to mention this to anyone at the lake, although he knew it was cowardly to let them remain in their suspended state of expectancy.

The girl with whom he was dancing chattered happily away as they pounded their noisy, footstamping path around the floor, and in spite of his miserable thoughts he tried to keep up with the conversation.

He was relieved to see Janey, together with a striking dark-haired older woman and a distinguished-looking gray-haired man, enter the hall. As soon as he could, he extricated himself from the clutches of his partner and hurried across the floor.

Janey was quite obviously glad to see him, and as he stood before her, he knew that she was undoubtedly the most gorgeous creature he had ever laid eyes on. Among the blue jeans, flannel shirts, and ginghams of most of the people present, she looked like a vision from fairyland with her sun-drenched, golden hair and her lovely mauve gown. The thought flitted through his mind that she was a little out-of-place, but then he heard the whistles and saw the admiring glances of the young men present. Although he hated being conspicuous, he could not help swelling a little with pride, because he was perfectly aware that the gown was in honor of him, for Janey's mother was dressed in riding breeches and a silk shirt and her mother's companion had on a pair of dark corduroy trousers and a checked flannel shirt. Pat began to wish he had put on a suit instead of his old faded denims.

But Janey held out her hand to him and greeted him with such enthusiasm that he forgot all about it. She introduced him briefly to her mother and their friend, a French actor with some unpronounceable name. Pat hardly saw them.

Then they were dancing together his arm tight about the small figure which seemed to fit so well against him. He suddenly realized, as she snuggled closer, that she was wearing very little, if anything, under her gown.

"I've got your shirt and your unmentionables out in the car," she said.

"Thank you."

"And…and thank *you* again for hauling me out this afternoon."

"Oh, please forget it. You don't want to remember that forever."

"Why not?"

"Well…well, I don't know. It can't have been very pleasant for you."

"It *became* very pleasant." She smiled at him and he felt her deep, demanding effect on him and again the thought that she was almost naked under her gown struck him. He saw her nude white body in his mind and he felt it against his own. He found himself breathing hard.

"Boy"—she grinned like a teenager—"was mother ever shocked when she found out that I had been buck-swimming with a strange man."

"You could hardly call that buck-swimming with a strange man."

"I don't know what else you could call it."

"Well, it wasn't voluntary anyway."

"That's true, I guess."

The music had stopped. They suddenly realized it and joined Janey's mother and her friend on the benches by the wall. Pat now took time to regard them. He found her mother to be an amazingly young-looking woman whose dark hair and flashing eyes seemed to be the very opposite of her blonde blue-eyed daughter's. He found it hard to connect the two in his mind. But Mrs. Hamsun was an extremely gracious and animated lady, charming and witty and entirely attractive.

The actor, whose name he finally learned to pronounce, was an eagle-faced, somewhat remote person. Pat suddenly observed with a start that he had seen this face before, in movie after movie, and realized that in his preoccupation with Janey he had practically ignored a celebrated star of stage and screen.

The thought went through his mind—*how can I use him?* And then he was ashamed of himself, but at the same time he had the reaction that comes to ordinary people when they meet a celebrity—a feeling of pride that the great person deigns to talk to them, a slight feeling of awe, a "feather-in-my-cap" sort of feeling. Rather than make an ass of himself, he put out his arms again to Janey as the band struck up once more.

As they danced they talked about everything and nothing. Their bodies seemeed to glide together with an inner rhythm made especially for them. During a moment of silence Pat suddenly heard Janey humming softly under her breath to the tune the band was playing.

"Like it?" he asked.

"Uh-huh. Very much. At college it's one of our favorite dance tunes."

"It's nice."

Janey laughed. "In fact, we have a kind of traditional song to it. That is, not we girls, but the boys do."

"How's that?"

"Well, they have a big school of forestry there. Every year the foresters throw a big ball. It's the biggest brawl of the year and all sorts of things happen. Well, the boys have a song about the girls in one of the dorms and a couple of the lines go like this…" She waited until the appropriate moment in the music arrived, then she sang, "… And when we go to the foresters' dance, we never ever wear any pants…" She laughed again. "Crazy, isn't it?" She looked up at him and there was a challenge in her eyes.

Pat swallowed deeply and held her closer. He didn't answer her. When the number was over he suddenly could not restrain himself any longer. He stopped by the door and drew her outside. She came willingly. He pulled her into the shadow of the trees and crushed her roughly against him.

Her arms went about his neck and clung like a vice and then her soft mouth was warm and open against his, her little tongue breaking gently through the barrier of his teeth. They stood like that for a long breathless moment, then his hand glided searchingly down over her hips, seeking a telltale edge.

"I didn't," she whispered laughingly. "I didn't wear any."

"Why not?" His voice was hoarse.

"Because. Just because."

"What are you trying to do?"

"Do?"

"Yes. I mean … what's on your mind?"

"You."

"Me?"

"Since this afternoon, nothing but you."

He crushed her closer against him. Then he laughed. "Do you know," he said, "after you left me this afternoon I was so excited I jumped for the boat and missed it and fell right smack into the water again."

"No!"

"Yes. That's how excited I was."

"Me too."

"What's the matter with us?"

"I know."

"What?"

"You gotta find out for yourself."

They kissed again and her hands caressing the back of his neck almost drove him crazy. They strained against each other, almost groaning in their need.

Then Pat pulled away. "Janey."

"Yes?"

"I know this is going to sound like a rotten question, but I've just *got* to know. I've got to know whether this is for real."

"What do you want to know?"

"You know ... that little song in there. That ... that come-on. That isn't just a line, is it? I mean that isn't ... I mean that isn't what you usually do, is it?"

She did not get angry. She became terribly concerned. "Was that why you were frowning?"

"I—I guess so. I was afraid of it."

She hugged herself close to him, boring her head into his chest. "Oh, you idiot," she whispered, "you dear, darling idiot. Of course it was a come-on."

He tried to pull loose, but she clung to him.

"Darling," she went on, "I knew when I was doing it that it was awfully brazen. I was a little scared of it myself. But I couldn't help it. Oh no, no! I have never done anything like that ever before. I guess I just wanted to sweep you off your feet. Maybe it was wrong to be so bold about it." She drew back from him and looked up into his eyes. "I love you, I love you, I love you," she said softly.

He couldn't say anything at all. They clung to each other for a long while, then he laughed, a little hysterically. "This is the craziest thing," he gasped and moved away from her, deeper in the the shadow of the pines. "This is the craziest thing that has ever happened to me. I'm in love. I'm in love at the nuttiest time for a fool to be in love!"

She followed him closely. "Why is it so nutty?"

He turned toward her and spread out his arms in a wide, helpless gesture. "I haven't got a bean. Not a thing. I have forty dollars between me and starvation and every picture I've sent in this summer has come back. I'm in no state to fall in love."

"What's love got to do with money?"

"Don't you want to eat?"

She was silent for quite a while before she asked, "Are you proposing?"

He turned away again, then he started briskly toward the dance hall. "No," he said curtly.

She ran after him and caught his arm. "You were too."

"No." He shook her off roughly.

"I don't care about money."

"I do."

"But I've got plenty of it."

He stopped and caught her roughly by the shoulders. "So what? So what? So what if you have?"

"So you don't need to worry."

"Oh, don't I? What do you think I am? A gigolo?"

"That's silly. That's a cliché. In all clean-cut wholesome American books, the hero always says this to the heroine when she suggests that they should use some of her money. It's the darndest nonsense!"

"To me it isn't nonsense."

"You really mean you don't want to marry me?" Her voice was very small.

"Of course I want to marry you!"

"Then what are we arguing about?"

"About money. I don't want to marry you until I can afford you."

"Oh," she sputtered, "oh, that's the ... the ..."

"I mean it. Not another word about marriage or anything until I can afford to talk about it."

"All right, all right!"

"I mean it, do you hear?"

"I heard you. I *said* all right."

He kissed her gently. "Please don't be mad at me, Janey. I've got to do it this way. Otherwise I wouldn't be able to live with myself. Okay?"

"Okay."

"Now let's go back."

They started back toward the hall when Janey suddenly thought of something. "Wait," she cried, and caught his arm again. "Just a second. Oh, why didn't I think of this before? You don't have to worry about taking any of *my* money. It's mother's money and you can *earn* it. You're a photographer and you can *work* for it."

"How's that?"

"Well, among her many other activities, mother serves as some kind of agent for theatrical performers. She is always in need of pictures of them. In fact, many's the time she has had photgraphers up here at the lodge to make pictures of one kind or another. She even has a darkroom and everything. I'll talk to her about it. Tony Ramova the dancer is coming tomorrow. Maybe mother needs some pictures of her."

"I'll get my own jobs, thank you."

Janey stamped her foot. "Oh, you *are* an idiot!"

"Maybe I am." He started away.

Janey caught up with him. "Please, please, please, Pat, don't get mad. Honestly. We just met each other this afternoon. We just discovered that we are in love tonight. We just now decided we want to get married. We don't even know each other yet. And now we have already had our first quarrel. How fast can you live?"

Pat laughed and hugged her close and kissed her. "You're right, of course. I wonder whether this is going to be one of those marriages where the wife is always right."

"Oh, no. I promise you. I'll pretend to be wrong every so often so that you can maintain your pride."

"Thank you very much, madam."

Nell Hamsun ran her eyes over the young man as he entered the hall with her daughter. The old familiar feeling came over her. Here we go again, she thought. I only hope that Janey's heart isn't too set on this one.

She considered the boy, her mind slowly tasting the fact that he and her daughter had been naked together that afternoon. He was an attractive youngster, all right. From his kinky, sandy hair and broad shoulders all the way down along his six feet to the bottom of his rolled-up jeans he was all male and all desirable.

She became aware that the actor at her side was watching her closely. "You keep out of this, Jacques," she hissed between her teeth.

"It's not fair to Janey, Nell. Every boy she has ever had, you have taken away from her."

"Keep out of it, I said." She advanced toward the young couple and held out a hand to Pat. "How about dancing with the old lady?" she asked.

"Old lady?" The boy laughed. "What old lady?"

"Me."

"Goodness, you must be all of thirty."

"Oh, yes, *all* of," Nell said drily. They danced away together. She put her arm around Pat's neck and moved very close to him. If he was surprised at her action he did not show it. A deep sense of pleasure coursed through her at the proximity of the young male. "You must come and see me ... *us* at the lodge," she whispered in his ear. "When will you come to see us?"

"Why, any time. I'd love to come."

"How about tomorrow?"

"Why ... why ..."

"There'll be someone there whom you might like to meet. A very beautiful dancer. Not old like me."

"I'd be happy to come tomorrow, and you're not old, Mrs. Hamsun."

"Please don't call me Mrs. Hamsun. It makes me feel so—so staid. Call me Nell."

"All right—Nell."

"That's better." For one more dance she managed to hang on to him Then there was an intermission in the music and she and Janey left the men to their own devices and repaired to the so-called "Ladies' Room," an outdoor establishment which, however, was clean and neat.

In the privacy and dimness of the little cell, Janey turned on her. "Don't do it again, mother," she said coldly.

"Do what, dear?"

"Don't try to steal Pat away from me the way you have all the others. The others didn't mean much to me, but Pat does."

"Why, honey, I don't know what you are talking about. I have only been nice to him in order to invite him to our house so that you may see more of him."

"You're lying!"

Nell was suddenly a hissing, spitting wildcat. "Don't talk to your mother that way, you ... you little ..."

"What?"

"Never mind."

"Bitch, mother? Were you going to say *bitch?*"

"I never use words like that."

"That's a laugh."

"I'm sorry you feel that way, Janey. Believe me, I have no intention of stealing your boy friend. As a matter of fact, I've invited him over tomorrow. Perhaps it would be better if you applied the energy you are expending on abusing me in thinking up some sort of entertainment for him."

They returned to the dance hall where the music was just starting again. Nell observed with a certain amount of glee that before Pat could claim Janey for the dance, the girl was claimed by one of the country boys, who swung her away over the floor in a sweeping waltz. Nell looked about for Jacques and found him thumping along with an awestruck dewy-eyed local matron. She smiled at the woman's expression and sidled close to Pat. "Too bad," she breathed in his ear. "Come on and I'll console you with a drink."

Pat cast a last, longing glance at Janey out on the floor and followed her out.

When they were seated in the rear of the Hamsuns' enormous Cadillac, Nell reached into a compartment in the seat-arm and extracted a bottle of Scotch. She extended it to Pat. "Help yourself. Drown your sorrows," she said.

"I haven't got any sorrows," he answered. "Here's to you, Mrs. Hamsun." He tipped the bottle.

"Nell," she said, and moved closer to him. It became abundantly clear to her that the proximity of her perfumed, mature body was having its effect on him. He looked nervous and uncomfortable. *I'll make him comfortable in a minute,* she thought. She held out her hand for the bottle and he handed it to her. She drank deeply and handed it back. "Have another."

"I … I think I've had enough."

"Oh nonsense, drink now. I'll be unhappy if you don't."

He drank again, this time more than before. She dropped a hand, as if by accident, on his knee. "You *must* come for cocktails tomorrow," she said. "The young dancer who'll be there is a very successful burlesque star. She likes to go swimming at cocktail time so that everyone can see her in her swimming-suit." She giggled. "It's the smallest swimming-suit you've ever seen." Then she added as an afterthought, "And she does have the loveliest breasts in America."

She was pleased to see the slightly glazed look with which Pat regarded her. She took the bottle from his hand and put it away. Then she turned toward him and put up her arms.

"Do you like *my* breasts?" she asked deliberately.

The boy gulped and drew back from her a little.

"Kiss me," she muttered, suddenly clamping her arms about his neck and planting her mouth on his. She gave him the full benefit of her experience, and although he was stiff and remote at first, she soon felt the unmistakable evidence that she was making an impression on him.

She began to run her hands over him in such a manner that he could not prevent it, for he never knew where they would alight next. His breath came more and more quickly. She pulled him closer and closer.

Suddenly he struggled loose and pulled back from her. "Mrs. Hamsun," he stammered. "Nell … I mean … hadn't we better go in?"

It was obvious that he was intensely uncomfortable and Nell smiled inwardly, although she felt as if his nearness and desirability had bored itself into her stomach like a sharp drill. "Don't leave me, please!" She managed a convincing little sob. "Please, Pat. You don't know what it is like to be old."

"You're *not* old."

"Oh yes, I am. I'm almost forty. You don't know what it's like to reach the middle of life and to be lonely and forsaken. Please hold me in your arms a little, Pat. That's not so much to ask."

She snuggled close to him and he reluctantly placed an arm about her. "Oh, I'm so unhappy, so unhappy," she breathed, her hands returning to his body again. This time her fingers were more insistent and soon she sensed his excitement and knew that even if he wanted to, he could not quit now. Her hands made sure that he would not want to quit.

After a while she felt him, at first timidly, then more aggressively, touching her breast. His fingers separated the buttons from the buttonholes and soon she knew them to be experiencing the full tautness that was her pride. She felt the points harden under his palm and her breath came faster and faster and mingled with his own.

Now there was no reserve between them any longer. If Pat had had misgivings when she offered herself up to him, they were gone now under the skill and insistence of her inflammatory technique. Her hands molded and stroked and caressed him madly and he was pulling the shirt down over her shoulders until she sat naked to the waist, her breasts, large and proud, shining in the faint moonlight. They no longer heard the music from the dance hall as the night and the moon and the world rapidly dissolved into nothing around their frenzied bodies.

He bent his lips to her breasts and she almost screamed with the agony of his teasing tongue. Then she felt his fingers at her belt, and hastily, nervously, helped him undo it. Her jeans loosened, and under his eager hand, both they and her white silk panties slid to the floor.

He started to lean over her, but she pushed and tugged at him until his face turned toward hers, incomprehension written all over it.

She smiled painfully—a hideous, lascivious grimace—and reaching out, grasped him by the hair and pulled him close. She threw back her head and gasped, and gradually the growing crescendo of her moans filled the car and she felt herself diving deep into the wonderful blood-red, seething ocean of utter oblivion.

CHAPTER THREE

Pat's dilapidated old Ford sputtered up the long macadam driveway to the Hamsuns' lodge the next afternoon.

He was in a strange state of confusion. He was tormented by a nagging sense of guilt over what had transpired between him and Nell Hamsun the night before. At the same time he had a hard time seeing how he could have avoided it without entirely alienating the woman. He was ashamedly aware of how useful she could be to him. He just couldn't afford to offend her, he told himself. But he knew that not only was that just an excuse, but it was a rather ugly, greedy, selfish excuse.

He thought of the strange irony of the day before. I meet girl. Fall in love with girl. Want to marry girl. She feels the same way. I do *not* make love to girl. I make love to girl's *mother!*

"If that isn't the damnedest thing," he said to himself. His mouth had a sour taste of self-disgust. He thought of Janey. How could he face her that day? Did she perhaps know? He and Nell had been gone a long time. Did she suspect, if she did not actually *know?*

He was aware of the terrible ugliness of his thought as he drew up at the front of the imposing entrance of the large house, constructed like a log hunting-lodge. He jumped out of the car and approached the front door. It opened and a very correct butler admitted him to the entrance hall.

"The ladies are expecting you, sir. They are at the pool. May I direct you?"

A very polite butler. He did not even glance at the rattletrap car. Pat followed him into the huge living room that featured one entirely glass wall opening out on the view over the lake and the mountain range beyond. Through the windows he saw that a well-groomed lawn sloped down to the lake shore. In the center of the lawn was a large kidney-shaped swimming pool. Apparently the lake was not good enough for Mrs. Hamsun.

The butler showed him through a glass door in one end of the enormous transparent wall, and he stepped out onto a flagstone terrace, well supplied with handsome and comfortable furniture. He started toward the picturesque swimming-pool that glowed in the bright sunlight.

There were three women at the pool. Janey, in a very chic riding habit, and her mother, in a pair of slacks that matched the aquamarine of the pool, were reclining in low chairs, a small table holding their drinks between them. Stretched out on the diving board was easily the most spectacularly beautiful woman that Pat had ever seen. She had flaming red hair and was dressed—or was the word really *dressed*?—in a tiny green Bikini sun-suit.

Pat was almost upon them, walking in the soft grass, before they were aware of his presence. Nell Hamsun jumped to her feet, followed by Janey, and held out a hand to him. "Pat! I'm so glad you could come. Janey has been simply on pins and needles for the last hour."

He looked uneasily at the blonde girl, but she gave no sign that she knew anything about what had happened in the car the night before. She only smiled and came close to him. She spoke softly. "Hello, Patrick."

He smiled uncertainly at the name, as if he were not sure it was an endearment, but perhaps a sign of coldness toward him. However, there was no coldness in her eyes and he breathed a deep, secret sigh of relief. A broad smile spread over his face as he decided to play his role to the hilt. He bowed a sweeping bow. "Good afternoon, ladies."

Nell took him by the hand and led him toward the red-haired beauty on the diving board. The woman sat up, and Pat caught his breath as he got a good look at her magnificent, tip-tilted breasts, barely covered by the tiny bra.

As they approached she arranged her mouth in a well-proportioned, carefully modulated professional smile. She did not bother to involve her eyes in the effort. They stared out, wide and cold and green, from under calculatedly obvious artificial eyelashes that were pearly with beads of black mascara. She held out a languid hand and before Nell got a chance to effect an introduction she drawled, "So pleased. So very pleased."

Then she lay back down again, seeming to pull up to her chin, like a blanket, one of the prettiest little Narcissus complexes ever displayed.

Pat almost laughed out loud. For through the velvet curtain of the liquid drawl had peeped the little gamin face of a good old-fashioned, genuine Brooklyn accent.

Nell grinned at him, and although he nourished a kind of loathing for her because of the séance of the night before, he rather liked the straightforwardness of her eyes and her grin and her way of talking. "This," she said, laughter in her voice, "is Tony Ramova, commonly known as 'The Torso.'"

"Please, my dear," drawled The Torso from under her fleecy blanket of self-love, "not *commonly,* if you don't mind."

"Oh, let her stew in her suntan oil." Nell grinned. "Come here and sit down." She drew a chair up to the little table and she and Janey and Pat sat down. She lifted a silver cocktail-shaker from the tray on which it sat and filled a glass with a beautiful, oily, pale-yellow martini. This she handed to Pat. Then she lifted her own glass and sipped. "Now, what do you have planned for the afternoon?"

"Well, nothing special, mother," Janey said. "We *could* go riding, I suppose. Or—"

Nell said matter-of-factly, "I'd like to talk to Pat about some photographic work, Janey, and this seems a good opportunity."

Janey looked doubtful. Pat turned toward Mrs. Hamsun, a big question-mark written on his face.

"Janey told me about you," said Nell in answer to his unspoken question. Then she turned to her daughter. "Be a good girl and run along for a little while and let me talk business with Pat. After all, it's in *your* interest, too."

Janey could not deny the logic in that. She smiled again, waved her hand gaily. "Well, all right. I'll be back after a while," she said. "Give him a *lot* of work, mother." She ran off across the grass and disappeared around a corner of the house.

Nell pressed a button on the table, and almost immediately the butler appeared on the terrace. Before he could come down to the pool, she called to him across the lawn. "Carson, bring us some Scotch and some soda and ice and take away this stuff." She waved a hand at the shaker. "It tastes like medicine," she said to Pat as he seated himself in the chair vacated by Janey.

The butler disappeared, to return a brief moment later carrying a loaded tray.

The Torso had not stirred during the entire scene.

When the Scotch was on the table and the butler had gone into the house again, Nell said, "You do the honors, will you, Pat?"

He proceeded to mix drinks as his hostess called to the young woman by the pool, "Hey, Tony, are you indulging?"

"In what?" came the languid drawl, and even in that brief question the voice was like two notes being played on a fiddle simultaneously, one sweet and delicate and the other sour as acid.

"In Scotch," cried Nell. "Come here and join us."

"Why didn't you say so in the first place?" asked The Torso, as if she had not heard Nell order the drinks from the butler. She unfolded her body slowly and gracefully, like an insect-eating plant lazily unfurling itself as it reaches for its prey.

"Fix half a tumbler on the rocks for the body there," Nell said to Pat. "She'll come and get it when she gets through adoring herself. And when she does you'd better have another one ready immediately. She swills this stuff like chocolate milk."

Pat fixed the drink. When he had finished he turned to hold the straight one out toward Miss Ramova. He almost dropped it when he saw the vision that floated toward him across the grass.

The Torso was not a tall woman, but she was built as if she were. Everything seemed long and slender about her and Pat thought of the old hackneyed phrase about long-stemmed American Beauties. Her legs were incredibly long and slim for her height. Her hips were small and her waist was even smaller. The only large objects about her were her marvelous breasts and her huge eyes, which stared vacantly and coldly from a small heart-shaped face.

If she weren't so phony, thought Pat, she would be the most remarkable creation on the surface of the earth. His eyes never left the gorgeous girl as she came toward him. She noticed him looking at her long, flowing, flaming hair and a genuine smile passed over her face.

With a surprising childishness, she sat down cross-legged on the grass by Nell's feet. She tilted the glass and emptied it in one draught. She held it out to Pat and he immediately refilled it. This time she took a small sip and looked up at him from under her incredible eyelashes. "So *this* is the boy," she murmured.

"This is the boy," Nell said.

The Torso kept her eyes on Pat. "Are you any good?"

Pat was flustered. What the hell did she mean by that?

"Oh, that depends," he said, a little too nonchalantly.

The girl laughed. "You got that one all wrong," she said. "Let's go back and start over again. I mean—can you take good pictures?"

"Oh ... oh, *that*." Pat felt like an idiot.

"Yes, that." She looked up at Nell and suddenly she was all Brooklyn. "Whassa matta with him? He stupid or something?"

Nell laughed uproariously. "As if you weren't aware of it, Tony," she gasped. "You're a little disconcerting, you know."

The redhead was greatly pleased. "No kidding, am I?" she asked of Pat.

"To say the least," he breathed.

She looked back at Nell. "You know what?" she said. "I like him. He's a good kid." Then she turned back to Pat again. "But can you take decent pictures? I don't mean decent," she added hastily, "I mean good. Could you make poor little me look good?"

Pat almost choked on his drink. "You'd break my lens."

"Help yourself to another, Pat," Nell said.

Tony was staring at him. "What's he mean by that?" she asked.

"He was paying you a compliment, dear."

"That's what I mean," said the girl. "He's a nice boy." She dipped her face into her glass again.

Nell said, "Pat, I've got a proposition for you. I like you—as you have undoubtedly gathered," she said meaningfully. "I want to do something for you. I'd like to keep you around for a while."

Pat was not too sure the conversation was going in the right direction. He took a deep swallow of his drink and kept his eyes noncommittally on the handsome woman.

"Besides, I need you," she went on. "I serve as a kind of agent for some young people like Tony here..."

The girl at her feet suddenly spluttered uncontrollably into her drink, spewing a little of it on her thighs as she lifted curving lips from the glass. Pat stared at her.

"Oh, she's right," Tony cried. "She's an agent. She isn't kidding you. Not her." She held out her empty glass and Pat filled all three again. Then, once again, he looked expectantly at Nell.

Mrs. Hamsun did not seem to mind the girl's outburst. She reached out an affectionate hand and pulled the flaming head against her knees. Tony settled back and an expression of well-being spread cross her features. Her eyes closed and a warm little smile played about her lips.

Nell went on, "As I was saying, I serve as an agent for various stage personalities like Tony here and Mr. Fribeaux who was visitng us yesterday. You remember him?"

Pat nodded. Of course he remembered him. How the hell could he forget him? One of the greatest stage personalities of the day and he had hardly had a chance to say much to him.

"Well, I can't be in that kind of business without pictures, as you probably know. Lots of pictures. Good pictures. I used to have a staff photographer, but he quit a couple of weeks ago. The position is open. Do you want it?"

"How do you know I'm good enough?"

"I don't. But I can find out easily enough. I have a darkroom on the place, and we have Tony here." She patted the girl's hair lovingly. "Suppose you make some glamour shots of her. You can turn them out in the darkroom and we'll see how you do. Is that fair enough?"

"I've never done much of anything like that."

"Do you mean to tell me you are afraid you can't make a good picture of *her?*"

"I don't know. I've never tried anything like it."

Nell stood up. "Go get your camera. That is if you have it in the car."

"I've got it."

"Well, get it and whatever other equipment you need. We'll have another drink while we are waiting."

Pat's gait was not the steadiest in the world as he went toward the house. "How the devil am I going to make pictures in this state?" he asked himself. When he returned to the pool, lugging his equipment, he found The Torso ready and waiting for him on the diving board. Nell Hamsun was deeply engrossed in her drink.

By now Pat had become intrigued by the assignment. He squinted at the sun and took in the layout of the pool. From his gadget-bag he chose a green X1 filter and a Pola-Screen. From the depths of the container he tugged three film-holders, loaded with Super Panchro-Press, Type B film. He was aware it was not the best film he could use for glamour shots, but it was fast and he intended to catch the bird on the wing.

Fitting his lens-shade with the X1 first and cramming a film holder into the rear pocket of his trousers, he said, "Okay. Let's see what we can do."

Tony Ramova stood up, posing prettily in the sunlight. "How's this?" she asked.

"Corny," he said. He looked around. A white towel was lying on the grass close to the edge of the pool, just as if someone had intended to go swimming. He knew quite well that The Torso had had no intention of getting her red curls or her postage-stamp suit wet. The others were dressed, so what the towel was for, he had no idea. But it could be used for a picture.

"Just a sec," he said. "Stay where you are on the diving board for a minute." The girl stood still and he maneuvered around, looking for an angle. Finally he was kneeling on the grass, close to the edge of the pool, the sun hitting Tony at a right angle to his lens. He reached into his gadget-bag again and drew forth a miniature flashbulb. This he fastened in the flashgun on the camera. From a back pocket he pulled a clean white handkerchief. He draped it over the gun, in order to diffuse the light from the bulb.

Then he was ready. He opened the ground glass at the rear of the camera and looked at the girl through it. Millimeter by millimeter he pulled her into complete focus. Then he lowered the camera, closed the ground glass and placed the film holder. He pulled the black slide.

"Take a good look at where you are standing," he said. She looked down at the board. "Get a sense of proportion into your head. You are almost exactly two-thirds of the way from the edge of the pool to the end of the board. Remember that. Remember it so well that when I give you the next instructions you will automatically keep that information at the back of your mind."

Tony checked her position carefully. He gave her plenty of time. Finally she looked up.

"Okay?" he asked.

"Sure."

"All right. Now this is what I want you to do. Come in here and get this towel." He pointed to the white towel lying on the grass behind him. "Then go over by Nell. Hold the towel behind you like a cape with both hands so that it seems to hang from your shoulders. Then run straight from Nell to the point on the board where you are now standing. As you run, open out your arms so that the towel is flying straight behind you. As you get to our spot on the board, whirl, still holding the towel out behind you over your shoulders. That's all you have to do."

Tony nodded, but he repeated the instructions to make sure that there would be no mistake. They went through the action to see how it would look. Pat checked the illumination with his light-meter, allowed for the additional shadow-filling light of the flash, and set his lens and speed. After he was through he said, "All right. Now let's shoot it."

Tony ran through the action again. In midwhirl Pat tripped the lens.

They tried it one more time, Pat instructing Tony to lean her body a little more in the whirl so that the picture would have a sense of action.

Then they went on from there. Using the Pola-Screen to cut the glare and darken the sky, Pat shot the red-haired girl from every angle—on the diving board, at the edge of the pool, on the grass, running, leaping, stationary. He went through eight film-holders before they quit. He had sixteen pictures. *Good* pictures, he thought.

He and Tony went back to Nell by the little table. She held out a drink for each of them when they approached. They downed them gratefully. She fixed another for each of them. Her eyes had a strange, glistening look and she looked from one to the other.

"Here, children," she said. "Have another. Have two others." She looked at Pat. "You know what you are doing, boy. But I'm not through with you yet."

Her voice was a little thick. Pat, excited by the picture-making and stirred by the two quick drinks, noticed that she was weaving a little in her chair.

Nell turned to him. "Have you ever made any nudes?"

He stammered a little. "Yes. Just a few here and there."

"Coeds?"

"Well, yes."

"Never anything like this?" She reached out and patted the thigh of the redhead who stood beside her. "Never anything professional?"

"No. Never anything like that."

"Well, you're about to. I want you to make some."

"Sure. All right." He took a deep swallow of the heady drink. "But why?"

"Because I want you to do it. Because I want to watch. Because I want to see what you can do."

The redhead laughed. "What's with you, coward?" she said to Pat. "Never seen a girl without her clothes on?"

Pat was indignant. "Sure. Of course, I have, but ... you don't understand. You're talking about photography. This is a problem"

"A problem?" Tony winked at Nell.

"Sure. You know, in texture and lighting and environment and lines and ... Hell, I don't know what!" He started to fold up his camera. "Maybe we'd better forget this,"

The Torso moved closer to him. "Oh no you don't. If Nell says *do,* we do. Look here."

Standing before him in the sunlight, she reached behind her and the tiny brassiere came off in her hands. Pat blinked and gulped. He had never seen anything like Tony Ramova's breasts.

For so small a girl, they were large, but in no way did they droop. They stood out from her small chest, firm and pointed and sharp, their tips pink and inviting.

"You like 'em, eh? I thought you might. Don't you want to take pictures of them? They're the prettiest in captivity."

"That's the truth," he muttered.

"Well, come on, let's go."

"Suppose people are watching us from the house."

Nell laughed. "If you're worrying about the servants they've seen worse things than this."

Tony reached to her side, her eyes teasingly on Pat. She undid a small button and started to slide the little triangular piece of material from her hips. He stared in fascination until the girl stood completely nude before him.

He reached for his glass and found that Nell had filled it while Tony had been undressing. Without thinking, he gulped the entire contents in one long draught. He staggered a little with the impact of the drink. He found that he was breathing with difficulty. He could not take his eyes off the girl and his stomach was contracted as if it was being squeezed by a strong fist.

He fumbled ineffectually with his camera. "Well," he muttered, "well ... let's get about it."

The girl turned her beautiful back on him and walked to the edge of the pool. Watching her walk like that was a considerable experience and it was quite a while before Pat was capable of setting himself into motion to follow her. She sat down on the edge, dangling her feet in the clear water, and leaned back on her hands. The position threw her magnificent breasts into bold relief. "How's this?" she asked.

"Fine, fine."

He knelt with the camera, almost automatically choosing a low angle that would emphasize the out-thrust curves. Just as he was about to take the picture, she said, "Wait a minute." She sat up straight again, and glancing over her shoulder at Nell, who was leaning forward tensely, her hands covered her breasts for an instant. When they came away again, the peaks stood out, sharp and taut. "They look better that way," she murmured, "don't they?" She resumed her original position, a little smile on her lips.

After a while Pat's nervousness and tenseness left him. He made picture after picture of the naked girl. The mood deliberately created by the two women permeated him like a heady warmth, stole into his loins and legs as a kind of exciting stimulus. The whole situation had a kind of promise in it that made him forget everything except the pleasure of the moment. It made him forget Janey completely.

When he ran out of film and cursed himself for not having brought more, Nell stood up from her chair. Her voice was hoarse as she said, "Put that towel around you, Tony, and let's go inside. I want to show Pat where the darkroom is so we can see what we've got."

They went inside, Pat's heart laboring in his chest. He walked unsteadily, but his mind was clear. So very clear. He knew what he wanted. There was only *one* thing he wanted now. And he knew what it was.

From the living room they went down a long hall lined with doors. Nell opened one. Behind it was a perfectly outfitted gem of a darkroom. "Turn those negatives out, Pat," she said. "When you get through we'll be in that room down there." She pointed to another door.

Pat nodded. He went into the darkroom and closed the door. It did not take him long to find what he needed. Choosing a DK52 developer because it was fast he turned out the light and went to work.

Twenty minutes later, he turned the light back on, left the water running to wash the negatives, and went down the hall to the door Nell had pointed out.

It turned out to be Nell Hamsun's bedroom. Tony was lying on the enormous bed, dressed in a white terry-cloth robe. Nell was at the dressing-table in a transparent negligee. Under it, clearly seen through the gauzy material, was a youthful panty-girdle and a brassiere.

Nell swung around and said, "Come in, Pat. Well, did we get anything?"

"Some pretty good ones, I think."

"Fine. Here, have a drink." She held a glass out to him and Pat took it gratefully.

Tony patted the bed beside her. "Come and sit down, little photographer," she drawled.

He went boldly to the bed and sat down.

"Did you make me look pretty?" she asked, stretching her lithe body luxuriously.

"Better than that," he said drily.

She put a hand inside her robe and he could see it molding and caressing her own concealed flesh. Her body twitched a little. "Do you know what they say?" she asked. "They say I have the most desirable body in burlesque. Do you agree?"

"If it isn't, somebody sure is hiding a gold mine."

"Isn't that the truth?" She smiled. "Isn't that the naked truth?" She turned over on her stomach. "But you know what? I don't like boys very much—isn't that tragic?"

"What do you mean?—you don't like boys very much."

"No matter how much they like me, I just don't go for them, that's all."

"I don't understand you."

She smiled mysteriously at Nell. "You will. Oh, you will."

Nell, finished with her hair, came to sit on the bed by Tony. She ran her hand lightly down the girl's back and stroked and patted her hips. Tony lay very still now.

The room was beginning to whirl before Pat's eyes. His body was filled with a seething excitement, but all the drinking he had done made it impossible for him to concentrate on anything for very long.

In desperation he lay back on the bed trying to keep a hold on his sense of equilibrium. But the position only made the whirling worse. He closed his eyes for a brief instant and cold sweat burst forth on his forehead. He clenched his teeth and fought the rising nausea.

He was only dimly aware of the two women in the room with him. They were like dim, floating shapes to him. They seemed to be waltzing together in the middle of the room. Then the smaller of the two stepped behind the dark one and lifted the negligee from her shoulders. The little redhead touched the older woman's back and the brassiere sprang from her breasts, which swung into freedom in wonderful prominence. Then her hands began stroking down from the woman's waist, gradually rolling away the girdle as they went, until the full body leaped forth into white and glorious liberation.

Pat closed his eyes dizzily as he felt the bed move and smelled the perfume of their bodies, but he could not keep from looking and finally he was up on one elbow, his eyes staring from his drawn face. Then he lay back again, every nerve in his drink-drugged body screaming for release.

He had never been so grateful for anything in his life when their hands reached for him.

He did not hear Janey calling from the living room. He did not hear Janey calling from the hall outside the darkroom door.

He did not hear the bedroom door open, nor did he see Janey as she stopped on the threshold, her face transfixed with horror and loathing.

He heard nothing... only the short, sharp, concise words that Nell hissed in his ear.

CHAPTER FOUR

Pat woke up slowly. His mouth tasted like the bottom of a birdcage and his head throbbed with a dull, insistent pain. He groaned and opened his eyes. The surroundings were still unfamiliar to him. The rich wallpaper, the thick carpet, the glass door that opened out upon a balcony overlooking the lake and the mountains. Even the face, the gray, drawn, dissipated face which stared back at him from the mirror over the dresser was unfamiliar. He wanted to disown it, but it glared back at him out of lusterless, deeply shadowed eyes with a malice and a hatred that frightened him, even though he was well aware that the face was his own.

Well, little college-grad, he said silently to the face, haven't we come a long way in a week? The face grinned sardonically. Well, little *artiste,* how's with your world-shaking art? The face answered, *"Cheesecake!"* And its lips twisted into a lascivious grimace that was supposed to be funny.

The only trouble was that it was not funny.

He dragged himself to an upright position and staggered to the bathroom where he helped himself to a stiff dose of bicarbonate of soda. He stuck out his tongue at the hung-over face in the bathroom mirror.

Everywhere you go, you meet yourself. It's as if you're continually doubling back on the same tracks. And what a thing to meet! Swimming and loafing and women all day. Drinking and women all night. Headaches and bicarb all morning. Hurray for the idle rich!

He returned to the bed and sat down on its edge. The house was silent. He felt as if he had spent the night in a mausoleum. He leaned forward and placed his head in his hands.

It was a week now since he had made the pictures of The Torso. Janey had not been at dinner that night. No one seemed to know what had happened to her, nor did anyone seem to care very much. It had been a weird meal, to say the least. Hardly any words were spoken between Pat and the two women. There had been a glutted, satiated atmosphere in the room and very little of the dinner had been consumed.

The next day he had moved into the lodge as a "house guest." At Mrs. Hamsun's urging, he had printed the pictures that day and they had been sent off. He did not know where, nor did he care very much. He was intensely uncomfortable in the house with the women and had started his visit by wishing that he were somewhere else, far away.

But it seemed as if he could not get away from Nell. She had raved over the pictures when she had first seen them—and to tell the truth, they *were* fine pictures. Their display of Tony Ramova's charms was startling, to say the least.

Two days after the pictures had gone off in the mail Tony had disappeared. She had gone on a "business trip," Mrs. Hamsun explained vaguely.

Ever since that first afternoon, Pat had seen very little of Janey. Somehow she had managed to eat at times when he would not be around and she seemed to be spending virtually all her time riding her horses. On several occasions he had gone down to the paddock to find her, but each time she had managed to elude him.

He had only the haziest recollection of how that fateful afternoon had wound up and at first he could not understand what had happened to Janey. When this puzzlement became too intense he realized that he was lying to himself. His dreadful feeling of guilt told him what was eating on Janey. Obviously she was perfectly aware of his adventure that day. And if that was so, he could hardly blame her for her attitude.

He shook his head and the pain shot through it like a bolt of electricity. What the hell had gotten into him lately? When Janey's coolness had gotten to be too much for him to handle he had said to hell with her. He was in on a good thing here. Becoming a successful theatre photographer through the aid of Mrs. Hamsun was nothing to sneeze at He looked about him at the luxury, the wealth, the comfort which money could buy and his envy and avarice grew day by day.

Sometimes, as he had this morning, he would look at himself in the mirror and wonder at the stranger that stared back at him. He would marvel at the transformation that one big temptation and one short week of having it shoved at him had wrought. All he knew was that there were two Pat Mulroneys now, where there had only been one a week before. One, full of remorse and self-loathing, already longing for the good uncomplicated days when he had been following a straight and decent path toward a fair living. Another, who had met a lovely young woman and fallen in love with her, and through this chance meeting had become involved in a morass of greed and lechery which he did not seem able to combat.

He tried to put some of the blame on Janey for leading him into the mess, but the attempt was no good. It was not her fault and he knew it.

It was his own. *Only* his own.

He lay back on the soft bed and stared at the ceiling. If only success and money and fine apartments and luxurious living did not beckon at him so. If only his background had been different so that they would not seem so important and so tempting...

A sneer settled on his face. Don't you feel sorry for yourself, though? What the hell do you think you are doing to Janey? She is no part of this.

He marveled at how she could have lived in this atmosphere for years and yet remained untouched by it. He wondered just how untouched she was.

Finally he got up. He put on his swimming trunks and a robe and went downstairs. Breakfast and maybe a dip in the pool might straighten him out a bit.

Nell and Tony Ramova were sitting at the table in the dining room. As usual, there was no sign of Janey. He expressed no surprise at Tony's presence.

Nell laughed when she saw him. "Well, look who arises from the dead," she cried. "Here, Pat, have a little hair of the dog. Tony and I have good news for you."

Pat did not answer. He went to the end of the table and sat down as far away from them as he could get. He took the proffered Bloody Mary and downed the sickening mixture of vodka and tomato juice. While he was gagging on it the butler brought his eggs. He looked at the slimy, jellyfish-like objects with extreme distaste. After a moment's hesitation he started picking at them.

Nell and Tony watched him with amusement. Finally the girl spoke. "Aren't you interested in finding out where I have been, lover-boy?"

He looked up at her with dull eyes.

Nell smiled. "We've really got him licked, haven't we?"

His fury and frustration welled up in him. "What do you mean, *licked?*"

Tony went on. "Now, don't get mad, Pat. Honest, we've got good news for you. You know what? You're by way of becoming quite the boy in theatrical photography. I've been doing very well in burleasque for a couple of years, but I've never hit the big time. And because of your pictures I've got a top New York nightclub offer and a chance to go into a real, legit Broadway show. Now what do you say to that?"

"What's that got to do with me?"

"Why, you knothead! If you can do that for me you can do it for others. Once other performers see those pictures of me they're going to come knocking at your door. That's what it's got to do with you."

Pat was becoming interested. He sat there, staring at the women over his eggs, the Bloody Mary gradually warming his innards and clearing his head. "Yeah?" he said slowly.

"Yeah," Nell minicked. "Come on, wake up! We're going to do great things together."

Pat was still a little hazy. "You mean the pictures actually made a real impression on somebody?"

"They certainly did. The reason I left so suddenly was that I got a telegram from each of two producers who had seen copies of the shots. They wanted to see me in person. Each, in his way, said that those were the most eye-catching glamour shots he had ever seen. That's what kind of an impression they made. You're *in,* boy. From now on nobody takes pictures of me but you. And I bet you it won't be long before a lot of other women say the same."

"How'd you like a nice big studio in New York?" Nell asked.

"And how am I going to get that?"

"I'm going to invest in you, that's how."

"Why? What's in it for you?"

"I need a photographer and you're the best. Besides, I like you."

"What do *you* need a photographer for?"

"Do you think that Tony's success is going to leave my pockets empty? Do you think that Tony is the only performer I have an interest in?"

Pat knew that he ought to be elated. He was made. It was not the field of photography that he had been aiming at, but it *was* photography and it appeared that he was going to be mighty successful at it.

Then why wasn't he elated? Instead of being "made," he had the feeling he had been had. He couldn't figure out why he felt that way. But it was an insistent feeling. He felt as if, somehow, he had been hooked. Besides, there was Janey. Would success bring *her* back? He knew better.

"Well, aren't you happy?" asked Nell. "Isn't this what you wanted?"

"I suppose so," he said dully and continued eating his eggs.

After breakfast he excused himself and went down to the pool. Nell offered to join him, but for the first time in their brief relationship he snapped at her, telling her curtly he wanted to be alone. She asked him sarcastically whether this was an artistic mood, and he left the room without answering.

He did not feel like swimming. Instead he lay down in the sun and closed his eyes. His mind was a whirlpool of confusion ...

Janey watched Pat from where she was sitting on her horse among the trees a hundred yards away. She watched him for a long time. Then she dismounted and walked across the soft grass toward him. He did not hear her and for a little while she stood behind him and looked at his motionless body.

She was in a state of utter perplexity. Ever since she had walked in on him and her mother and Tony that afternoon a week ago she had not known whether to hate him or not. Knowing her mother better than Pat thought she did, she was fairly sure that the major portion of the blame for the incident did not lie with Pat, who would at best have been a complete babe in arms in the face of her mother's wiles. At the same time the sick feeling of disgust and disappointment would not leave her and she could not see the boy she loved without seeing also that ugly scene.

Although she had only the vaguest notions of the machinations of her mother's business ventures, she did know something of her nocturnal habits. She had lost too many boy friends to her mother's insatiable hunger for the conquest of youth, not to be thoroughly familiar with that aspect of the older woman. However, the sinister implications of Pat on the bed with both her mother and Tony were new to her. She did not understand them, but she knew that what had just taken place right under her very eyes went a lot deeper and had a much more significant meaning than her mother's earlier coquetries.

She asked herself whether all of those earlier flirtations had ended up like that. The fact that she had never caught her mother in such a situation before did not mean that such things had not been going on. She thought back over the several times she had lost a boy friend because of her mother. They had never been too important to her, for there had always been more where they came from. Janey had never lacked for male attention. But now she realized that all of the occasions had followed the same pattern. After once having fallen under the spell of the mother none of the boys had ever sought the daughter out again. In fact, they seemed to have studiously avoided her, as if they had committed something shameful that made it impossible for them ever to face her again.

Janey thought she knew what it was now, and as she stood there watching Pat, her love for him strong within her, she wanted desperately to save this one relationship above all the others. She approached quietly and put a hand on his shoulder.

He jumped as if he had been pricked with a needle. "Oh," he said. "Oh, it's you." He turned his head away.

"Yes, it's me," she answered.

He did not look at her. "Where've *you* been?" he asked.

"Around. Thinking."

"About what?"

"About us."

"What about us?"

"I don't know what about us. *You* tell me." It made her sick to watch the shamed twitching of his handsome face.

"I don't know what you mean."

"I think I ought to tell you. I walked in on you and mother and Tony the other afternoon."

He got up abruptly and moved away. So she *did* know. Well, that was that. He figured that put a stop to anything they might otherwise have had together. Well, in that case he might as well put a bold face on it. "So?" he asked curtly.

"So don't you want to say anything to me about it?"

"You want it described in detail?" Oh, how he loathed himself, but the shame was so strong in him that all he seemed able to do was lash out like a wounded rat.

"Pat, Pat, Pat! What's the matter with you?" She came toward him anxiously, her hands reaching for him.

He knew if she touched him he would break down and bawl like an infant. He backed away. "Nothing's the matter with me."

"You know this isn't you talking. And what happened the other day was not the real you either."

"How do you know? Altogether you've only known me for a few hours."

"Why do you want me to believe such a thing?"

"I don't want you to believe anything."

She turned away from him and spoke into the air. "Are you in love with my mother?"

He tried to laugh, but the sound that came from his throat was nothing but a rasping croak. "Don't be ridiculous."

"What about Tony, then? Are you in love with her?"

"No!"

"Then what are you doing?"

"Look," he said, twisting uncomfortably, his eyes everywhere except upon her. "What business is it of yours? Leave me alone, can't you?"

She spoke quietly. "Of course I can't, Pat."

"And why not, if I may ask?"

"Because I love you."

There was a long pause then. Finally he sat down on the edge of the pool, his back to her. "Forget it, Janey. Forget it."

She had never heard so tired and so lost a voice. She knelt by him. "I can't forget it," she said and tried to touch him.

He jerked away with a violent wrench. Then for the first time he looked squarely into her eyes. "I'm *using* your mother, Janey," he hissed. "I'm using her for all she is worth. The pictures of Tony were a great success. I can't quit now and I can't use your mother and still maintain any kind of relationship with you. Unbelievable as it may seem to you after the past week, what little decency I have rebels against everything about the whole arrangement, but I don't seem to be able to help myself. So leave me alone."

She pulled back from him. "You don't mean that."

"I mean it."

"You could go so far with your photography without this."

"How do I know? Anyway, I can go there a hell of a lot faster this way."

"But what about you? What about what you are doing to yourself? And to me?"

"You have no hold on me, Janey."

She stood up then and stared wide-eyed at him.

He bowed his head and muttered, "I can't help myself, Janey."

"You can't help yourself!" She was blazingly angry now. "You can't help yourself, you say. What kind of man are you? A softspoken, polite, well-mannered college-boy one minute—a greedy, ambitious, depraved...oh, I don't know what, the next minute. And a stupid fool on top of everything. Don't you know my mother and Tony are a whole lot smarter than you in this sort of thing? Do you really think *you* are using *them?* I don't know what's on their minds, but I guarantee that when all the chips are down you will discover that it is *they* who are using *you* and not the other way around!"

"Go away and leave me alone," he said wearily.

"Don't worry," she screamed. "Don't you worry. I'm on my way."

As she ran toward the house the image of beautiful Tony Ramova was before her eyes. Somehow all her fury and all her hatred and all her sorrow became focused on the woman who had posed for the fateful pictures that had started Pat off on this rampage. She wanted to kill her! No, rather than that, she wanted to disfigure her so badly that she would never be able to draw advantage from the pictures, that she would never be able to pose for another one, either.

Janey ran through the living room, hurtled down the long hall, flung a door open and leaped into Tony's room.

The red-haired girl was there. She was dressing and had just finished pulling the dress over her head. Before she got a chance to turn around Janey was upon her, her hands hooked like claws.

She grasped the neck of Tony's dress from behind and ripped straight down. The garment tore clear to the bottom hem, the two halves falling over the girl's arms and hampering her movement.

Tony cried out and swung about, facing her infuriated attacker. "What do you think you are doing?" she yelled, but before she could say anything else, Janey had raked her nails across the beautiful face, leaving long, scarlet streaks along both cheeks. This time Tony screamed with pain and her hands flailed futilely as the torn dress prevented her from covering her face.

Janey was babbling incoherently. "I'll ruin you!" she stammered wildly. "I'll tear the flesh from your bones. I'll scar you for life. You bitch. Oh, you bitch!"

Tony managed to release her arms. The dress fell away as she fled madly across the room, trying to get some furniture between herself and Janey. She was now dressed in nothing but the sheerest black net underwear and her white skin gleamed through the garments.

Her obvious beauty infuriated Janey even further. She leaped after the girl, turning over furniture as she went. Great, wracking sobs were rasping from her gaping mouth. Her eyes rolled madly in her face.

As she again flung herself on Tony her victim managed to fling her arms about her. Her hands caught at the back of Janey's riding shirt and it was torn from her shoulders until it hung in strips about her waist.

Janey continued the struggle, dressed now in a small, white brassiere, breeches and riding boots. She bent the redhead back over the bed until she lost her balance and both tumbled onto its softness. With one hand free, she ripped the black brassiere from the beautiful, upthrust breasts. Then she tried to rake her nails across one of them, but Tony rolled out of the way, Janey's own brassiere coming off in her clutching hands. Janey's round breasts sprang into view, trembling and stirring with the violence of her agitation.

Tony drew back a fist and hit with all her strength. Janey cried out and cowered on the bed. The dancer, with catlike speed, swung off the bed and caught up a table lamp. She jerked the plug from the socket in the wall in one and the same movement and lifted the weapon over her head. But Janey came in fast, under the uplifted arm, tackling the other girl about the middle. They both fell to the floor.

By now Janey's intention merely to disfigure the redhead had gone out of her mind. She wanted to hurt her. She wanted to hurt her so badly that she would be squirming and leaping and screaming with pain. She threw herself with all her weight on top of the other girl, her fingers digging at her belt buckle. Tony was stammering out desperate demands for an explanation of the violence, but Janey clenched her teeth, her fingers working with lightning swiftness to pull the belt from its loops. Finally she succeeded, but just then Tony broke from under her and ran for the door, her large breasts leaping and bouncing as she ran.

Janey was after her in a flash, her hands reaching out before her. They caught in the elastic of the black net panties. It ripped with a small, hissing sound and the little garment came off, leaving Tony completely naked.

Janey caught her about the knees and brought her down with a crash. But the sweat was pouring off both of them and it was hard to hang on. Holding the redhead down with one hand, she managed to get to her knees. She lifted the belt above her head and brought it down across the lovely, soft white hips. Tony's body leaped off the floor with the pain. Janey hit her again and as Tony tried to roll out of the way she stood up and rained blows on the cringling, crawling, twisting body.

The leather strap left long, red welts on the soft flesh, crossing and criss-crossing until the girl's back looked as if she had been clawed by a panther. Janey's sobs were mounting as she struck and struck and struck.

Tony was almost silent after a little while. She had started screaming, but the screams quickly turned into little moans each time her body quivered with a new blow. The room was quiet now, except for Janey's sobs, the hissing and slapping sounds of the belt whining through the air and striking flesh, and Tony's little gasping moans.

Finally Janey's arm grew so weary she could no longer lift it. She dropped the belt on the floor and sank down on the bed, her face hidden in her hands. Her weeping did not subside.

Tony lay for a long time quietly on the carpet, her pitifully bruised body throbbing and trembling. After a while she stirred, wincing with the pain. She raised herself laboriously to one elbow. "What the hell was that for?" she muttered.

Janey did not answer.

"What have I ever done to *you?*"

Janey remained silent. She turned away and let herself fall on her stomach on the bed, her face buried in her arms.

Tony looked long at the white, quivering back. Then she stood up with pain-wracked difficulty. She sat on the bed and put a gentle hand on Janey's shoulder.

"For heaven's sake, honey," she said quietly, "what's the matter with you?"

Janey kept on weeping.

Tony slid her hand along her back, feeling the sweat that glistened there. "Look, honey," she said. "Suppose you tell me later. Right now you know what both of us need? We need a nice, soothing bath—that's what we need. Here, let me help you." She stood up and gently disengaged the waist of Janey's riding breeches. She pulled the boots from her legs and took the breeches off.

Janey lay passively weeping. The panties she had on were dyed purple.

Tony winced audibly when she saw the color. She pulled them carefully from Janey's hips. Then she did a strange thing. She bent over and with an incomprehensible combination of tenderness and passion she kissed the trembling back between the shoulderblades. "You poor kid," she muttered. "Something's gone all wrong with you."

She went into the adjoining bathroom and started the water running. Then she returned and lifted Janey from the bed. She led her into the bathroom and helped her into the warm tub. Then she got in herself.

She soaped her hands and began running them gently over Janey's body, around her neck, down along her arms and flanks.

Gradually the sobs subsided and Janey found herself leaning back against Tony. She felt a very pleasant, and at the same time vaguely shameful, warmth creep over her. She did not even attempt to explain to herself what was happening. She lifted her arms a little and Tony's soapy hands slid over her.

After a while Janey was breathing deeply and quietly, resting softly in the tender arms. Finally she spoke. "I ... I don't know what came over me," she said softly. "Somehow, it was all your fault."

"What?"

"Oh, Tony, I wish I knew. Something terrible is happening—to Pat, to me ... to mother, to this house. I don't know. Something is all wrong."

"And you thought it was my fault?"

"Yes."

"Why?"

"You posed for those pictures."

"Is that all? Is that what you jumped me for?"

"I ... I guess so. It seems awfully foolish now."

"Do you want to make amends?"

"I guess so. I ... I know it sounds stupid, but I *am* sorry."

"That's not what I meant. If you want to make amends, do to me what I just did to you. Those welts are sore!"

They changed places and Janey's small, soapy hands slid gently over Tony's back, along her arms and down her legs.

At last Tony turned her loose and stood up. "Here's one for you," she said, stepping out of the tub and handing a large towel to Janey, who followed her. "And one for me." She took one herself and started drying Janey, who in turn began gently to rub Tony's body dry. When they were both through, they were a glowing pink and their young bodies were warm and their flesh seemed to have a tender, yielding quality to it.

Janey thought she had never felt like this in all her life. Embarrassed, she went into the bedroom to retrieve her clothing.

Tony followed her. She lay down on the bed and said, "Now, Janey, come here and tell me what this was all about."

Janey sat timidly on the edge of the bed and tried to explain. Then reality seemed to fade away, leaving nothing but softness and velvet, deep-breathing silence and a warm, moist cocoon ... and then the whirling concussion of multicolored fireworks exploding in a black midnight sky.

Pat sat staring thoughtfully into the water of the pool for a long time after Janey left him. He had attained what he had set out to get—the start of a photographic career. In some ways it was, of course, completely different from what he had intended. This was hardly what you could call "nature photography." Or could you? On the other hand, the financial remuneration it seemed to promise far outstripped anything he had considered, even in his wildest dreams.

He gritted his teeth. It had *better* have some real money in it. The price he was paying for his career was something he did not want to think about.

Nell Hamsun sat down in the deckchair beside him. "I want to talk to you," she said.

He nodded and waited.

"You have proved yourself to me," she went on. "Tony was telling the truth when she said the people she talked to were impressed by your photographs of her. Now—I've got a proposition for you. I want you to listen carefully and I want you to remember that what I am about to tell you is to be kept in the strictest confidence. Is that clear?"

He nodded again, his eyes on her face.

"Whatever business arrangements pass between you and me are never to be anyone's concern but yours and mine. Okay?"

"Okay."

"All right then. This is my side of the proposition. I will set you up in a modern, well-equipped studio in a fashionable part of New York. I will send all of my picture business your way. Through my theatrical clients you will meet others and in that way you can expand your business. In return for this I will not ask anything of you but an eventual return of the money I have invested—plus a few favors."

"Favors?"

"Yes. They will be professional favors. By that I mean that now and again I may ask you to make some special pictures specifically for me and not necessarily along your usual line of work. Do you agree?"

"I don't know. I don't understand what you are talking about."

"It is not necessary that you should. All you need to do is take the pictures when I ask for them."

"What kind of pictures?"

"Oh, various kinds. Being a sort of agent for stage performers is not my only source of income. I have other angles, and the pictures to which I am referring will be along those lines."

"But can't you tell me what they are?"

"You'll find out in due time."

Pat sat very still for a long while. Finally he said slowly, "You have already done a lot for me, Nell, and I'm grateful. Without you my outlook at the present time would be pretty black, to say the least. You are offering me a career, readymade. You are staking me to a regular life of luxury. Why?"

"I like you, Pat. You know that. Haven't I proved that?"

"Is that *really* why?"

"Not entirely. You are a good photographer. I need a good photographer. But more than anything else I need a photographer who will do what I want."

"And what is that?"

She smiled. "And one who will do it without asking questions."

"Nell, I've got to be honest with you. I don't like this. I don't like to agree to something I don't know anything about."

She stood up and moved a little away from him. "Pat, look around you. Do you like this pool? The lawn? The lake? The house? The drinks? The furniture? The paintings? The beautiful women?"

He hesitated. "Well, yes," he finally said.

"*You* could have everything I have and perhaps more within a very short time. You are young. You are lucky, because you can begin at the top. Doesn't that mean anything to you?"

"Well, yes, I suppose it does."

"You suppose? Would you rather be going hungry? Waiting, hoping, praying that some editor will deign to accept a picture of yours?"

"No."

"Instead, you can make plenty of money and enjoy the luxury of decent living, with plenty of leisure to pursue your own photographic interests. Is there anything in the world to keep you from developing your abilities along those favorite lines of yours during your leisure time? And eventually, in comfort and with a full belly, become so good at it that you cannot be denied by an editor? We all have to begin somewhere, Pat. It seems to me that I am offering you a rather superior way to make your start."

He saw the logic in what she was saying. "You're right," he said. "Okay. I agree."

She returned to her chair and sat down beside him. "Good. I'm glad you see the light." She drew a sheaf of folded papers from the pocket of her slacks. "Now I want you to do something. I have always found, even when I am working with personal friends, that a businesslike agreement on paper is better than just a word-of-mouth one. Sometimes even among the best of friends difficulties can crop up. It is always better under such circumstances to have a clear-cut contract. Don't you think I am right?"

Pat nodded. "I expect you are. I've never had much experience with things of that kind."

"Well, then. I want you to sign this paper. Just as a formality, of course."

Pat took the document. It was several pages long and was enfolded in the blue cover of a legal paper. He started to read it.

Nell produced a pen from her pocket and held it out to him. "Here, you can use my pen."

"Just a minute. I kind of like to read what I am signing."

She spoke archly, as though it was a joke. "Don't you trust me?"

He looked up in surprise. "Of course I trust you. Shouldn't I?"

"I was just making a joke, you silly."

He smiled and returned to his reading. The document appeared to be just an ordinary legal contract, starting with the usual "party of the first part" and "party of the second part." With many judicial embellishments, it went on to describe the arrangement to be arrived at between the two parties, concerning the establishment of a carefully described photographic studio, etc., etc.

Suddenly Nell stood up. She reached for the papers. "Wait," she said urgently. "I just thought of something. We haven't got a minute to spare. Never mind the contract. You already know what it is about by now. You can sign it later." She practically snatched it from his hands.

He looked up in surprise and she went on hurriedly. "This is more important than signing that silly thing right now. I want to talk to you before Tony gets up from her nap. There's something I want you to do for me. It's the first of the special assignments I mentioned."

"Yes?"

"Yes. Now listen carefully. Tomorrow morning we're going to have company. A young lady of whom I am very fond is coming to spend a couple of days with me. While she is here I want you to make some pictures of her. Will you do that?"

"Why, certainly." He was amazed at the simplicity of the request.

"It isn't as easy as it sounds, Pat. She is quite camera-shy. You may have to endear yourself a little to her to persuade her."

"Hell, if she doesn't want her picture taken, why force it on her?"

Nell answered coldly. "That doesn't concern you. Will you do it?"

He could see no harm in it. "Sure. Why not?"

"Good boy. Now"—she put a hand out to him—"come on and let's go have a couple of lunch drinks." She pulled him up, and together they started back toward the house.

As they went he said, "You really are the strangest woman, Nell. Why are you so mysterious? All this about special picture assignments and secrecy, and I don't know what else. Why is it all necessary when it concerns such a simple thing as taking a picture of a camera-shy girl?"

She did not answer for a little while, then she said quietly, "Because I want them nude."

CHAPTER FIVE

atta Martinez arrived the following noon. Judging by her
clothes and her Cadillac, it was obvious to Pat that she was no
pauper. Nell greeted her effusively, as if she were a long lost friend.

Matta turned out to be a very pleasing damsel. In stature she
was not much taller than Tony Ramova, but there any resem-
blance ceased. She was the typical Latin-American, an olive-
skinned, raven-haired beauty with a fine acquiline face and
small, boyish hips and long slender legs. Moreover, she was a nice
girl. She smiled readily and when she spoke she made sense in
her soft, gently accented voice.

Pat liked her immensely. He liked her frankness. He liked
her too damned much to make sneaky pictures of her.

After the girl had had an opportunity to freshen up and get
herself settled in her room, the whole party met on the terrace for
drinks. It was a strange company, to put it mildly.

Tony bubbled and drawled alternately, not in the least affected
by the events of the past few days. Janey sat by herself, her face
tense and white, her eyes turned in upon her own thoughts and
her expression indicating that what she saw did not please her.
Pat was silent, a little embarrassed. It seemed to him as if the net
into which he had gotten himself was constantly drawing closer
and closer about him.

Nell poured over with charm as she soaked her handsome
visitor in a continual stream of small-talk. Pat had to admire the
older woman's exciting talents as a hostess. She really was charming and witty and clever. Even under the strained circumstances

it was a pleasure to listen to her. Matta merely smiled and nodded and joined in now and again, apparently entirely unaware of the tension in the air around her.

As the drinks began to loosen tongues, Pat noticed Tony sidling up to Janey. It suddenly struck him that it was the first time he had ever seen the redhead without a sunback dress on. Her body was entirely covered, and although it did not register clearly in his mind, he realized that there was something vaguely strange about the way she moved. It was as if in some unaccountable way she had hurt herself. Every movement she made had a certain gingerliness about it.

However, his attention was focused primarily on Janey. He saw her move away from the dancer as if in deep embarrassment. She turned her back and pretended to be completely engrossed in her mother's conversation with Matta. Tony shrugged her shoulders stiffly and moved away.

Pat kept watching Janey while he maintained a certain aura of attentiveness each time Nell or Matta directed a remark at him. *This is my fault,* he thought. *I'm the reason she is so unhappy.* But he knew he was committed now and he tried to shrug it off. She's a big girl, he told himself. If she doesn't like me, she doesn't have to sit for the rest of her life with her hands in her lap. She can have all the suitors and all the choice she wants.

Eventually they ran out of ice-cubes and Pat volunteered to get some more. He was returning from the pantry when Janey met him in the little hall.

"Pat," she said urgently, putting a hand on his arm. "Pat. Please, Pat. Don't do this to us. I'm sorry I ran off yesterday. More sorry than I can ever tell you. If I'd had any sense at all I would have stayed right with you no matter what had passed between us. Please, can't we talk this over?"

"I'm sorry, too, Janey," he said. "There's nothing I can say. I have committed myself on a long chance. I've got to follow through now."

"Why? You could become a wonderful and a very successful man without doing this. Why?"

He felt the frosty silver ice-bucket in his hands. He held it up and regarded it as if it were a symbol. "Because of this," he said.

She looked at him, not understanding. "What do you mean by that?"

He turned away from her. "I don't know, Janey. I'm in deeper than I care to be. But I'm in. Can't you understand that?"

"I don't understand any of it."

"I mean—well, instead of starting at the bottom and slaving and sweating and going hungry and being afraid, I can start at the top. I can start with a fine studio in New York and a good career all laid out for me."

"Are you willing to trade *me* for that?"

"That's not a fair question, Janey. No such bargain has ever entered my mind."

"But it's what you're doing, all the same."

"Don't you remember what I said the night of the dance. I said I didn't want any talk of marriage or anything else until I can afford you."

"You can afford me."

"Not the way *I* want to afford you."

"But what ... *what* is it that mother is offering you?"

Once more he held up the ice-bucket. "This," he said. "And this will lead to more, and perhaps some day I will be in a position where everything is right for us. I'm aiming at that, Janey. I'm going to work for that." Then he turned away from her. "Right now I'm a little dirty. I'd rather not talk about it." He went past her and she stood by herself in the hall, the tears running down her cheeks.

When he stepped out onto the terrace Nell waved to him to join her. She was deep in conversation with the two girls. They were talking about dresses and about the preservation of youth.

Nell stood up. "Put that bucket down and look at me," she said gaily. It was quite obvious that she had had a little more to drink than she could hold.

He put the bucket on the table and watched her. She turned her back on the assemblage and bent over slightly. The black slacks tightened and Pat saw the lines of the small panties that covered her slender hips under them. She straightened up again and turned. She threw back her shoulders and her magnificent breasts stood out in bold relief. "Now how about that?" she asked proudly. "I am no longer a young woman, but by careful living I think I have managed to maintain a certain youthfulness."

They all agreed and Tony asked slyly, "What do you mean by *careful living?*"

"I mean taking care of myself—exercise, maintaining a youthful attitude, being careful what I eat." Then she smiled and winked at Matta. "Drinking good liquor and getting plenty of loving. Isn't that right, Pat?"

Pat was beyond being embarrassed. "Sure," he said, "and then some."

Nell laughed. "Well, fix us all another drink, you lazy boy."

She sat down again while he went to work. When he had handed out the glasses he became suddenly aware of Matta's alcoholic state—the slight glazing of the eyes, the vacantly happy expression on her face.

"Have you noticed this boy, Matta?" Nell asked.

The Latin beauty turned her eyes curiously on Pat. He felt them burning into his flesh as she regarded him.

"I can recommend him," Nell went on, smiling through half-closed eyelids.

"He is quite an athlete. Stand up, Pat," she commanded.

He rose and she continued, "Now walk away from us."

He walked out upon the lawn, carrying his glass with him. Behind him he heard Nell whispering, "Look at those solid muscles. Wouldn't you just love to dig your nails into them?"

He turned around and came back.

Nell said, "Take your shirt off, Pat. Come on, take it off."

He obeyed, after draining his glass to the bottom. Tony took it from his hand and went to fill it again. He stood there, naked to the waist.

"Look at that beefcake," said Nell. "Come over here, Pat. Now Matta, give me your hand. Feel that muscle."

The dark-haired girl's fingers curled once lightly about his right bicep, then she let go and ran her fingertips lightly along the arm. Her long nails scraped delicately and left long pink streaks behind the trailing fingers.

A shudder ran through Pat. He looked up and saw Janey outlined in the door to the living room. She stood staring at them, disgust and loathing written on her face. Then she turned and disappeared from sight.

The fingernails suddenly dug into his arm and he glanced down. Matta was looking up at him and the invitation in her eyes was obvious.

He started to put his shirt back on. As he was struggling with it Nell caught his eye and nodded her head slightly. He took a deep breath and went to sit down by Matta. He bent forward and took one of her hands in his. Nell stood up, and taking Tony by the arm, she strolled away a little as if in deep conversation.

Matta looked at Pat. "Yes?"

"Look," he said and swallowed painfully. "Look. I'm a photographer. I'd love to make some pictures of you…"

"Of me?"

"Yes."

"For goodness' sake, why?" Her modesty was not put on. She really could not understand why anyone should want to make pictures of her.

"Because I think you are the most beautiful thing I have seen in ages. That's why."

"Really? You really mean that?"

"I certainly do."

"But that is ridiculous. I am just an average girl." Then she added a little wistfully, "You should see my mother."

Now Pat understood her modesty. Quite obviously here was a situation not unlike that of Nell and *her* daughter. He smiled and the smile was genuine now. "I'm not interested in your mother."

"You really want to make your pictures of *me?*"

"That's right."

"Oh, I don't know. I don't like very much having my picture taken. I don't think I shall let you."

"Please." He called to Nell. "Nell, will you tell this young lady that I am a good photographer?"

Nell grinned. "He's the best."

"Well, I don't know. I shall have to think about it." Matta shook her head.

"Okay. You think about it, but I guarantee you that I won't let you alone until you give me permission."

"But you flatter me."

"It is not flattery."

"What kind of pictures?"

"Oh, just pictures. Portraits and in dresses you like to wear, and ..."

"And ...?"

"Oh, maybe a bathing suit or something."

"No. No, that you shall not do. I am brought up in Argentina. In Argentina young ladies of good breeding are not photographed in their bathing suits."

"Well, you think about it."

She smiled. "I. shall. And thank you so much for wanting me. I am very proud."

He could not remember when he had been so touched. The girl was exquisitely beautiful. By all rights, she should be arrogant and throwing her weight about and rubbing in her physical beauty. But not this one. This one really did not think there was anything unusual about her. He felt like a dog and hurriedly downed his drink and went to prepare another one.

Tony returned, and stopping by Matta she said in her best Broadway voice, "Shall we go and prepare ourselves for dinner, my dear?"

Matta nodded. She rose and with a polite little nod toward Nell, she murmured, "You will excuse me, please?" Then she and Tony went into the house.

Good grief, thought Pat, she even has manners! She even his deference toward her elders. Then he smiled inwardly. He wondered whether Nell had caught the tribute to her age.

His conscience told him that he simply could not talk this girl out of her clothes for pictures that went completely against her grain. When he and Nell were alone on the terrace, he said, "I can't do it, Nell. She's a sweet girl. Her entire upbringing would rebel against such a thing. Even if I were to talk her into it, she would be sick with shame while she is doing it, and for weeks afterward—maybe for the rest of her life."

Nell smiled. "Come here with me," she said. She preceded him into the house, through the living room and dining room into the cubbyhole which she called her "office." When she had nodded him into a chair by the large desk, she started to rummage through a drawer. Finally she came out with two things. One was a bundle of clippings, the other was a couple of letters.

She held the clippings out to him. "Look at these."

They were fashion photos advertising the wares of an extremely exclusive dress shop in the city. The pictures were magnificent work, but the gowns were even more impressive.

"How do you like them?" she asked.

"They're fine. They're beautiful. So what?"

"So let me tell you something you don't know. Once last year I was in very dire straits. There's no need to tell you what was the matter, but what I want you to know is that it was Matta Martinez who saved my neck. If she had not there is no telling where I might be today. Not here, certainly. And not in the fortunate circumstances I now enjoy, either. Well, I owe Matta something. I owe her a lot and I want to do something for her. Something nice."

"Yes?"

"I want to present her with two of these dresses."

"What's that got to do with pictures?"

"You heard us talking about dresses when you came out on the terrace a little while ago?"

"Yes. I heard something to that effect before you started to show off your fanny."

Nell smiled. "It's not such a bad fanny, is it? Anyway, we were talking about these very dresses. I said I thought Matta had the kind of figure that could wear one of them. She said she could never do it."

"Why, for heaven's sake?"

"These things are virtually molded on you, Pat, that's why. They are fitted to your naked body. Well, Matta is in love with them, but she simply hasn't got the guts to go to a dress designer—no matter how much she adores his work—and strip for him so that he can build his work right on her flesh."

Pat was beginning to see the light. "But can he work from a picture?"

"He says he can. I'm going to get the most minute measurements of her on some pretext or other and the designer says that with those and pictures of her figure, he can do just as well as if she were actually there."

"But why, for heaven's sake, don't you give her something that is simpler than all this trouble?"

"I want to give her something very, very personal. What she did for me was personal. This is something she would never get for herself."

"I see."

"But two things, though, Pat. She mustn't know what we are up to or the whole surprise would be spoiled. And you must get pictures of every angle of her figure so that the designer can see every nook and cranny. Is that clear?"

"I still think this is a mighty peculiar way to surprise somebody."

"Remember you are working for me. Don't let your private opinions get in your way." She held the letters out to him. "You might like to read these, by the way."

He opened them. They were letters to Nell from two different agents. They praised Pat's work to the skies and begged her to put them in connection with him so that he might do the same for their clients as he had done for Tony Ramova.

When he was through he looked up. "Why didn't you show me these before?"

"Oh, I thought I'd hang on until I needed them for a little persuasion sometime. You understand, of course, that I have written both these men and told them you will have a studio in the city very soon and that they will be able to contact you there. I am sure you also understand that the pictures you will be taking of Matta, even though they have nothing to do with business as far as I am concerned, are strictly business as far as *you* are concerned. There's a thousand dollar fee in it for you."

"You don't need to do that, Nell. It's too much. You've done enough."

"You're working for *me,* Pat. You get paid for your work." She stood up. "Now let's go and get ready for dinner." Then she stopped. "Don't turn down my money, Pat. You'll need a lot of it to equip that studio."

Janey was not present at dinner. Pat felt her absence keenly, but he was rapidly developing a talent for drowning his regrets and his need of her in the luxury and the liquor that surrounded him. He and the three women drank freely during the meal.

Afterward as they sat on the terrace with their coffee and liqueurs, he was filled with well-being.

As it drew darker Nell deliberately turned the conversation toward sex and toward the sexuality of women. Pat could see that the drink and the talk was having its effect on Matta. Her eyes were shining and her cheeks were flushed. Her hands fluttered ineffectually when she gestured and she appeared to be moving uncomfortably and restlessly in her seat.

They drank more and the evening wore on, an aura of abandon and sensuality gradually settling over the company. Pat was getting very drunk, and the atmosphere on the terrace and the three women who were creating it were beginning to tell on him.

When the terrace was illuminated only by the faint light from the living-room lamps shining through the glass wall, Nell stretched her legs and stood up. "I wanna do something," she said drunkenly.

Tony lurched to her feet. "What?" she cried. "I'm game for anything!"

Matta looked at them, her head lolling just the slightest bit.

"How about you, Matta?" asked Tony.

"I don't know. What do you want to do?"

Nell straightened up. "I wanna compare legs. Okay?"

"Okay," echoed Tony. "Okay, Matta?"

"I don't know."

"Whatta you mean, you don't know?" asked Tony. "You got legs, ain't you?"

"I don't know."

Tony laughed uproariously. "How d'ya like that, Nell? She ain't sure."

Nell turned toward Pat. She lurched a little. Pat thought it looked a little overdone. He suspected it was an act. "You be the judge, Pat," she said. "I go first."

She came out into the middle of the floor and hoisted her skirt. Up, up it went, past her knees, up along her thighs, past the top edge of her sheer stockings, revealing white, full thighs, each lined with two black garters. On up the skirt went until it was bunched above her hips and she stood revealed in a tight black panty-girdle. She had beautiful, long, slim legs with dimpled knees. Pat, through his hard-breathing excitement, marveled at the youthfulness of this middle-aged woman.

"Okay, Pat? Seen enough?" He nodded and she dropped her skirt. "Who's next?"

Tony stood up. "Me! I am!" She took the center of the floor and started raising her skirt. Her legs were nude and as the skirts ascended, gradually revealing the wonderful velvety white of her rounded knees and slim thighs, Pat forgot everything and leaned forward. At the top of her thighs, she hesitated. She looked around and smiled.

"All the way up, Tony," said Nell. "I did."

With a sudden jerk, Tony pulled her skirt clear up around her waist.

She was not wearing any panties.

With a laugh she dropped the skirt. "Fooled you, huh? Gave you a cheap thrill, huh?" She went back to her chair and sat down. "Now you, Matta," she said. "Your turn."

The dark-haired girl shook her head a little and muttered, "No, no, no."

Tony jumped up and pulled her up by the arm. "Aw, come on. Nell and I both did. Come on. Don't be scared, nobody is going to bite you."

Matta looked about her. Everyone was regarding her with breathless expectation. All the tenseness seemed to cow her a little and she went slowly to the center of the floor. "All right, a little bit," she said. Neither her gait nor her tongue was steady.

She timidly raised her skirt to her knees. She was not wearing stockings and the slim rounded calves were pulled beautifully taut by the enormously high heels of her shoes. At the knees she stopped. She staggered a short step forward as she bent over to look at her own legs, but caught herself in time and stood there, swaying slightly, her skirt raised a couple of inches.

Nell was leaning forward now, her eyes riveted to the Latin-American girl's legs. Tony said, "Come on, higher."

Matta looked up and the sudden motion of her head almost threw her off balance. "I have never done anything like this before," she said miserably.

"Well, come on, there's gotta be a first time for everything."

The girl slowly raised her skirt a few inches farther, revealing gleaming, dusky thighs. Pat, himself deadly intent, could hear the deep breathing of Nell from the other side of the terrace. Everything was quiet except for the soft soughing in the pines that lined the edge of the lawn.

Tony whispered, "Farther."

Matta closed her eyes tightly and pulled the skirt higher. Her thighs had a beautiful full forward curve to them that cut back in just above the rounded knees. Pat could just make out in the darkness an almost microscopic soft dark fuzz on the ivory skin, like the fuzz on a peach.

The tears were beginning to roll down Matta's cheeks. "Don't make me do it," she pleaded. "I am afraid. I have never done anything like this in all my life."

Nell's voice came gently from behind her. "Are you a virgin, Matta?"

The girl nodded miserably. Tony started to hoot, but a swift movement from Nell stopped her cold.

"I am a Latin-American lady," said Matta softly. "We are very sheltered."

"Higher," gritted Tony and now her voice was hoarse.

Matta looked miserably at Pat, then she looked over her shoulder at Nell.

"Must I?"

Nell nodded, her eyes gleaming. "Tony and I did. Don't be afraid."

Matta closed her eyes again, tightly, so that little crinkles formed at the corners. Slowly, slowly she began lifting her skirt again. Pat and the two women waited breathlessly. When the bottom edges of her panties showed, she hesitated once more. She stood for a moment, swaying, undecided. No one said anything. Then, in the breathless silence, the skirt started upward again, and finally she stood revealed. Her little white panties were almost transparent.

Nell said softly, "Turn around."

The girl turned until she was facing her. The older woman's face gleamed whitely in the darkness, her eyes shining like a cat's.

Tony stood up. She went to the trembling girl and released the skirt from her clutching fingers. She let it drop back down into place. "That's enough," she said. Suddenly she kissed Matta on the cheek. "You win," she said. She led her back to her chair and held a drink toward her. "Here," she said. "You need this."

In the silence that followed, Pat rose and went to his room. He gathered together his camera, film and flash equipment and returned to the terrace. He put the armload on a table and looked at Matta, who was smiling now and laughing.

"Okay?" he said, "may I?"

She looked at Nell and Nell nodded. Matta laughed. "Such *things* I am doing tonight," she said. Then she looked at Pat. "All right. What shall I wear?" But before he could answer she interrupted herself. "No, no, I know. I know what I shall wear." She got up and hurried into the house.

Pat poured himself another stiff drink. Nell rose and went inside and he lifted his glass to Tony and toasted her. "Here's to the great cult of nudism," he said. They drank together and Tony came over and stood close to him and he breathed her perfume and thought of what he had just seen. He grew impatient. "Hurry up," he muttered between his teeth.

Tony laughed. "She'll get here. Don't get nervous."

After a while he heard a noise at the door behind him. He turned quickly and almost dropped his glass. Matta was there. She was wearing a white strapless evening gown that glittered with thousands of little pearls. Her black hair was piled on top of her head. "All right?" she asked. "You like it?"

"Do I *like* it?" He was completely stuck for anything else to say.

"Where shall I stand?"

Pat looked around quickly. The drink and the night and Matta made his head whirl. His hands trembled as he picked up his camera. He saw that the moon was out. He checked the focus-spot on his flash-gun. "Down by the edge of the lake," he said.

She nodded and started out across the lawn. Pat started to pick up the rest of his stuff to follow her. He was suddenly breathless with urgency.

"Just a second, Pat." Nell's pleasant, quiet voice sounded behind him.

He turned impatiently.

She was holding his contract out toward him. "While I think of it, sign this, won't you? I hate to have it lying around. I forgot it earlier."

"Later," he said, "later."

"It'll just take a second. You've already read it. Here's a pen."

His impatience was mounting. "All right," he said. "All right. Give me the pen." He quickly scrawled his name at the bottom of the last page, grabbed up his equipment and hurried after Matta Martinez.

By the edge of the lake he carefully arranged his model so that both her head and the gorgeous gown would be shown off to the best advantage, placing her so that the moon was behind and above her. Then he put a tripod far to one side. On the top of this he clamped an extension flash-gun which was plugged into the gun on his camera. Carefully feeding out the extension cord, he stepped slowly backward, looking through the ground glass on the back of the camera. When he was at the right distance, he pressed the button for the focus-spot. A small pinpoint of light

THE FIRE THAT BURNS

fell on the girl's bosom. He focused on this. Then he straightened up in the moonlight and checked the composition. It looked good to him. He loaded the camera, pulled the slide and shot the picture.

The procedure was repeated many times. He had to shoot the pictures quickly for the girl was swaying a little with drink. When he was through he crossed the grass to her. She was standing with her back toward him, looking out over the water.

"It is very beautiful," she murmured.

"Not as beautiful as you."

She turned toward him. "You are nice," she said. "I like you."

Suddenly he felt her hands on his arms, the fingers digging gently into his biceps.

"I like you very much," she whispered. She stepped a little closer. "Well?" she asked.

Then she was in his arms and her full, red mouth opened around his lips and he felt the little wet tip of her tongue. Her hands were running frantically over his body.

He slid his hand slowly down her back and as he did she clamped her hips closer against his. Suddenly she jerked her hips away with an abrupt, surprised gasp. But she came right back, grinding herself against him, her breath coming in moaning little cries.

"Tonight," she moaned. "Tonight! I shall come to your room tonight. Oh, darling. I don't even know what to do. You must show me. I want to find out. I want to find out about this wonderful thing. I am not afraid any more."

Pat felt the slender body writhing in his arms and almost screamed with his desire for her. Instead—feeling like a heel while he did it—he whispered in her ear, "Will you do something for me first?"

"Anything, oh, anything."

"I want to take some … some …"

She laughed against his throat. "Some pictures of me, of just *me*—is that what you mean to say?"

"Yes."

She pulled back from him. "All right, darling, but then you must help me." She held out a foot to him. "Unbuckle my shoe."

He knelt quickly before her and undid both shoes and removed them from her small feet. They had incredibly high and sharp heels. He stood up. "Why do you wear them so high?" he asked.

She giggled. "I don't know. I like them that way. She took one from his hand and pressed the spike heel into his solar plexus. "Look"—she laughed—"it is like a pointed weapon. Perhaps like a knife." She dropped the shoe and turned around. "Undo the zipper," she said softly.

With trembling fingers he pulled the lock down to the small of her back.

She hung on to the gown with her arms and turned again to face him. "Now!" she murmured. She let the gown slide slowly down. It glided to her waist.

There it hung. She was still covered by her arms. But now she let them drop to her sides and stood before him, naked to the waist. Her breasts were everything they had promised to be, proud, pointed, firm, not too large and yet not too small. They stood from her chest, their dark points trembling.

She stood like that for a moment, then she bent forward and pulled the dress from her hips. It fell about her feet and she stepped clear, her little naked feet flashing in the moonlight. She was dressed only in the sheer nylon panties, which he had seen once before that evening. With feverish movements her hands rolled them downward over her hips. Then they too slipped along her thighs and fell to the ground.

She was naked. Like a slim ivory column in the moonlight. A column shaped like a young woman with gleaming, rounded surfaces and deep, dark shadows, with black, glinting hair and wet, scarlet lips.

She stood before him without a trace of shame. "Go ahead," she whispered.

His hands were shaking so badly that as he took pictures of her from every imaginable angle he was afraid her image might be blurred on the film.

CHAPTER SIX

Early the next morning Pat went to the darkroom. His eyes were bloodshot from lack of sleep. He was exhausted, but he could not wait to see what his pictures of Matta looked like.

He had certainly not wanted to become so involved with her. Then, with a cynical smile, he realized that he was lying to himself. Of course he had wanted to get "involved" with her. From the very first moment he had seen her, he had wanted her.

He thought of Janey, but Janey was gliding away from him now. So many things had happened. He saw only too clearly that he was a young, inexperienced boy in the grip of forces he could neither understand nor control. Janey was a powerful part of the forces, but he was no longer capable of thinking clearly about her. So many things had happened to him. Things he had been too weak to combat. He was being dominated and he was following like a lamb led by the nose.

It did not make him like himself particularly.

Over a period of only a little more than a week he had met and become enmeshed by two super-experienced women. During that same time he had also met and fallen for two entirely innocent girls. Both had offered themselves to him with complete honesty and abandon ... and he had betrayed them both.

He felt like spitting on himself. Then he thought of the night before—of taking the pictures of Matta, of returning to the terrace and nodding a silent answer to Nell's questioning look, of going to the darkroom, his hands trembling with eagerness. He thought of Matta's soft knock on the darkroom door a little later, of the way she crushed herself against him in the darkness after he let her in. He heard again the frantic whispered promises in his ears and felt her hot, wet tongue against his and her searching, questing hands. And with a dreadful thrill he relived the moment later on when the door to his bedroom softly opened and her figure in a white, diaphanous negligee slipped through the narrow crack, closing and locking it behind her. How she had rushed to his bed, tearing the robe from her shoulders as she ran, how she had hurled herself at him.

He relived again her wild, choked breathing and the moist heat of her nudity, her gasping plea for solace and her strangled little scream when it happened. And her madly thrashing body!

Trying desperately to blank out the bewildered mess of guilt and confusion in his mind he put the first negative in the enlarger and began to print the pictures.

When he had finished printing, washing and drying them, he put them in an envelope and took them to Nell's little office. She was not up yet and the room was deserted. He placed the envelope on her desk and returned to his room, thinking of the prints he had just made. They were good pictures all right, although he felt that they did not do justice to Matta. He was not satisfied with them. There was a kind of frankness about the nudes that made them a little raw. Considering the circumstances under which they were taken, that was not too strange.

When he got to his room, he removed his clothes and went back to bed. He was very, very tired …

It was three o'clock before he woke up again. He felt a lot better. He reminded himself that the pictures he had made of Matta the night before had, after all, been for a good and kindly purpose. In the face of the way he felt about Janey, it was not so easy for him to forgive himself for what had happened with Matta *after* the pictures. However, he refused to castigate himself for it any longer.

He got up and dressed and went down the hall and into the living room. The house appeared deserted. He looked toward the pool and saw Tony down there, lying in her usual position on the diving board, her Bikini barely covering her beautiful body. He smiled and went on out to the kitchen to see if he could scrounge up some food. There was no sign of Janey anywhere, nor was there any sign of the servants. He looked in the refrigerator, got out some eggs and bacon and put them on the big electric stove.

He was sitting at the table, smoking a cigaret and drinking a final cup of coffee when he heard the door that led from the dining room to Nell's office open and close. Then he heard the murmur of voices from the office. There was only a thin wall between the little room and the kitchen, and after a while he began to distinguish occasional words of the conversation. Then, as the voices were raised slightly, entire sentences became audible. He listened, transfixed, to the little unseen playlet.

Nell: Well, here they are. How do you like them?

Matta: Oh, I did not know the gown was so beautiful.

Nell: Just look at those pearls glisten.

Matta: He is a very fine photographer.

Nell: He's more than that to you now, isn't he?

Matta: You ... you know?

Nell: Of course I do. Oh, don't look so distressed. I'm not going to tell anyone. Was it worth it?

Matta: Very much.

Nell: You're not sorry?

Matta: No ... oh, no. Always, I have wanted to know. Now I know.

Nell: And ...?

Matta: It is very beautiful. He is very kind ... and gentle.

Nell: He is very young—and so are you. I envy you. Envy you both.

Matta: Why should you? *You* have everything.

Nell: Have I? Now look at the other pictures.

Matta: Oh!

Nell: You are very, very lovely.

Matta: But so … so … naked!

Nell: That was the idea, wasn't it?

Matta: But they show everything. But everything!

Nell: They do that, all right.

Matta: Please—give them to me so I can destroy them. They frighten me.

Nell: Just a minute.

Matta: No, no, please. Suppose someone should *see* them!

Nell: Suppose someone should.

Matta: Please give them to me.

Nell: Not just yet. Please sit down. *Sit down,* I said!

Matta: All right. I am sitting. Now, please give me the pictures.

Nell: In a moment. I'd like to talk to you first.

Matta: Yes?

Nell: Yes. This may come as something of a shock to you, so make yourself as comfortable as you can.

Matta: Shock?

Nell: Do you remember how and when we first met?

Matta: Oh, yes, indeed. It was at Tiffany's, was it not?

Nell: It was. Do you remember what you were doing?

Matta: I think so. I was buying a trinket of some sort.

Nell: Trinket! It was a ruby pendant on a platinum chain.

Matta: That's right. I remember.

Nell: You call that a trinket? It cost fifteen thousand dollars.

Matta: You're right. It *was* a little expensive.

Nell: Then later we met again at Gina Andrews' cocktail party. You remember?

Matta: Yes, I remember.

Nell: You were wearing a diamond bracelet that must have cost forty thousand dollars.

Matta: No, no. It was not that much. Thirty-two thousand it cost. It was a present from my father. But Nell, what is all this leading up to? I would like very much to destroy those pictures.

Nell: How much?

Matta: I do not understand you.

Nell: How much would you like to destroy these pictures?

Matta: How much?

Nell: Exactly. Oh, don't look so startled. The world is full of people like me. We make it our business to get to know nice rich little innocents like you. What else do you think I would want with you?

Matta: I ... I thought you were my friend.

Nell: I am. Oh, I *am!* I am so much your friend that I let you have my favorite boy last night.

Matta: Your ... your ...?

Nell: Do you think that if it weren't for business reasons I would have exposed that boy to you? Don't you think that I am aware that with your looks and your youth you could take any boy away from me, no matter how experienced and skillful I am? Do you think I enjoy knowing that? Do you think it is fun to sit here and get older and older and older every day? To see my place as a woman usurped by little girls with fresh faces and tight little bodies? To fight my daily battle against the wrinkles and the sagging skin with creams and ointments and lotions and face-masks and mudpacks and massage? Do you think that is fun?

Matta: Nell! Nell, you're mad! You don't know what you are saying.

Nell: Shut up, you driveling infant. Look at you, sitting there. Butter wouldn't melt in your mouth. Look at those tight little cantaloupes sticking out from your chest. Do you know how many times I have had plastic surgery on my breasts to keep them from hanging like potato sacks? Three times, *that's* how many. And you sit there, sniveling and puling, with the safe, secure knowledge that you're desirable. Well, that I can't take away from you. But one thing I can take away from you is some of all that money you're flaunting around. The pictures and the negatives will cost you one hundred thousand dollars.

Matta: One hund—!

Nell: And if you're not interested in making a deal they will be spread all over South America. *After* your father has received *his* copies, of course.

Matta: I...I...I do not have one hundred thousand dollars.

Nell: Then get it!

Matta: But...but...Nell...Señora Hamsun...

I...I do not understand this. Surely you are joking. We are friends, are we not? You were so kind in the city. I met so many nice people through you. You helped me get away from my mother a little. You invited me up here. You promised me that we should—what did you say?—"loosen the stays a little" here. Last night I was scared, yes, but it was not bad. It became very beautiful. I was very, very grateful to you for what you had done for me. It is not good to live like a child. Out in the world, yes, but like a child, because one is an Argentine lady. Why did you do all this? Because of *this*? Because you wanted to trick me? If you need money, why did you not just ask me for some?

Nell: *Beg* you? Is that what you mean? I don't need to beg to get money.

Matta: This way is better?

Nell: Never mind! Just get the money. When it is in my hands, you get your pictures.

Matta: And the negatives?

Nell: They stay right here with me.

Matta: I won't do it!

Nell: Suit yourself.

Matta: Why not the negatives?

Nell: Do you take me for a fool? If I turn everything over to you, what is to prevent you from going after me with the police?

Matta: And if you keep them you can always threaten me again later, when you need more money.

Nell: I could, but I won't.

Matta: How do I know that?

Nell: You don't; you will just have to take my word for it. Even *I* have a peculiar sense of honor about my dealings.

Matta: The honor of a thief. Of a crook. Of a sneaking ... rotten *blackmailer!*

There was the sound of a furious struggle in the other room. Pat had been welded to his chair in complete horror at what he heard. Now, suddenly, he was galvanized into action. He flung back his chair and rushed into the dining room and tore open the door to the little office.

The two women were struggling in the middle of the floor. He leaped into the room and tore them apart. Holding Matta by the arms from behind, he pulled her back toward the door. She fought like a tigress.

Nell swung toward the desk and he shouted at her, "Leave those pictures where they are!" He released Matta and ran toward the desk, but he was too late.

Nell caught the prints and the negatives up in one sweeping grab, flung them into the wall safe, slammed the door and whirled the knob, all in one great movement. Then she stood there with her back against the safe, a little smile on her lips. "I had not intended for you to find out quite so soon," she said.

"Give me those pictures. Open that safe and give me those pictures!"

She shook her head. "They're too valuable to throw away. Don't you want your studio in New York?"

"I don't want anything with that kind of money, you ... you unbelievable bitch!" He started toward her, his hands outstretched like claws.

She did not move an inch. "I wouldn't if I were you," she said. She was looking over his shoulder at something in the door.

He spun around. Carson was standing there, a little snub-nosed automatic in his hand.

"I don't believe I'm going to need you, Carson," Nell said calmly. "Just stick around out in the dining room for a little while. Close the door after you as you go out."

Pat stopped in the middle of the floor. He turned toward the black-haired girl. The tears were running down her cheeks. He started toward her, but she turned away in silence.

"Matta," he stammered, "Matta, believe me! I knew nothing about this. I took the pictures because she sold me some cock-and-bull story about a designer who was going to make you some dresses. They were to be a present from her. And because I wanted to. Because you were so beautiful. Believe me."

"Get away from me," the girl said quietly.

Nell said, "Come now, Pat. Don't tell me you really fell for that story. You knew what you were doing. Don't try to lie about it."

He whirled on her. "You shut up!" he cried. "You just shut up! We're finished, you and I, but before I go you're going to hand over those pictures."

"I don't think so."

"You'll do it, all right." He started toward her again.

"All I need to do is raise my voice and Carson will be right here with his little gun."

"Do you really think I'm going to let you get away with this? Suppose I really let you extort this money from Matta. The minute she has those pictures I'll blast you wide open."

"I'll still have the negatives."

"You won't get a chance to use them. I promise you that! You'll be hit so fast you won't have time to turn around."

"Not by you, I won't."

"You wait and see."

"You're mine, boy, lock, stock and barrel."

"Not any more, I'm not!"

"*Now* more than ever."

"How do you figure that?"

"You signed a contract, remember?"

"You're crazy! That paper doesn't include anything like blackmail. You can't get me on that."

Nell opened the drawer in her desk and drew a sheet of paper out. She handed it silently to Pat. He read it, his mouth hanging open.

I, Patrick Mulroney, hereby admit and confess that, of my own volition and acting entirely on my own initiative, I have taken nude pictures of young women. I have used these pictures successfully for purposes of blackmail and extortion.

signed ....

He looked up in bewilderment. "Do you think you're going to get me to sign this?"

"You have already signed it. As you will notice, this is only a carbon copy. And the original now lies snugly in another safe."

"This is not what I signed." Pat was getting frantic. His voice rose. "What I signed was a plain ordinary contract."

"I intended for you to think that. But as you may now remember I did not give you an opportunity to read the last page. *This* was the last page. Here are the others." She reached into the wastebasket.

He recognized them instantly. Slowly he crumpled the page in his hand and tossed it on the floor. Then he turned back to the girl. "I don't know what to do, Matta," he said. "I don't know what to do. This woman is so fiendishly clever, I can't fight her."

She did not answer him. He turned back to Nell. "So now what?" he asked.

"So now Matta pays up and all you have to do is be a good boy."

He looked at Matta and said, "Matta, please believe me. I didn't know anything about this. Please, please believe me. And please forgive me."

The girl stared at him, her eyes cold and unblinking. He turned and stumbled blindly from the room. In the dining room he encountered Carson, who grinned at him and handed him a bottle of Scotch and a glass.

"Take this," said the man. "It helped a lot when she got her hooks in *me*."

Pat took them and went on out on the terrace. He went past the pool and on down to the lake. He was in water up to his knees before he realized it.

He waded back and sat down on a rock. He filled the glass to the brim and drank it down. The liquor hit him with a painful shock.

An hour and a half later he was still sitting there. With the help of the bottle he had managed to reduce reality to a hazy, expressionistic distortion. The trees around him seemed to be shuddering, rattling skeletons—deathheads staring at him out of cold, empty sockets. The rocks about his feet were little leering faces, grinning at him with lascivious, twisted, blubbery lips. The lapping of the water on the shore whispered lewd words to him as he sat desperately digging his fingers into his face, leaving huge purple bruises on his cheeks and about his eyes.

He was incapable of thinking. In a weak, whining voice he cursed himself over and over and over. *This* he had come to. In ten days of being a stupid and unbelievably gullible fool.

Where was Janey? He suddenly stood up. The bottle fell from his lap and shattered among the rocks. He flung the glass violently out into the lake. Janey! Only Janey could save him now. Only Janey could give him back his sanity.

"*Janey! Janey!*" He called her name and started staggering toward the house. He stumbled and fell down. He got up again and half-crawled, half-dragged himself toward the house. Finally he managed to get on his feet. He started running a crazy zigzag course toward the terrace.

When he stumbled into the living room, he headed for the hall, crashing into furniture and dragging down lamps as he went on his erratic course. "Janey!" he screamed. "Janey!"

He came to her door and flung it open. The room was empty. He looked about frantically. Everywhere was evidence of a hasty departure. Clothes were thrown helter-skelter on the bed. The closet was open and so were the bureau drawers. The signs were eloquent.

Janey was gone…

He whimpered like a puppy and started back out of the room. "Janey," he muttered. "Janey. Help me, Janey." In the doorway, his knees buckled and he slid to the floor, his fingers clutching the door frame, his forehead against the cool wood. "Janey," he whispered.

Suddenly he felt a light hand on his shoulder and hope flared up in him. He looked up, expecting to see the familiar blonde head. But instead the head was red. He looked into Tony's eyes, the tears running down his cheeks.

"Come along with Tony, honey," she said in a soft voice. "You can't sit here like this." She lifted him to his feet and led him along the hall to his room. When they were inside, she locked the door and helped him to his bed. He dropped upon it as if every bit of energy, every ounce of resistance, had been drained from his body.

When he opened his eyes again, Tony was there, bathing his face with a cold, wet cloth. He lay inertly, watching her through half-closed lids, not caring about anything.

She laid the cloth on the night-table and put her hand on his forehead. "Better?" she asked.

He nodded weakly.

She leaned over him. "Honey," she said, "you mustn't let it get you so."

He asked weakly, "Did you know that this was what was in her mind?"

She looked away. "Not entirely," she said. "Oh, I knew she had done it before and I knew she would do it again." Suddenly she looked earnestly at him. "She's crazy, you know," she said. "Completely nuts. She's panic-stricken by her age."

"Has she always been like this?"

"I don't know. I haven't known her that long. All I know is that she was married to a very successful man—a *good* man, too, they tell me—and she just simply drove him out of the house when she had had Janey. She accused him of preferring the baby to her. She accused him of all sorts of horrible things. Of course there wasn't a word of truth in it. But she drove him out of the house anyway. They say it was a perfectly filthy divorce case. She managed to win custody of Janey and that was that. She's crazy, I tell you."

He nodded. "Yes, crazy. And she's driving *me* crazy too."

"Well, I know how you feel, but you might just as well take what she offers. You can't get away from it now."

"But ... *blackmail!*"

"You had no way of knowing. You're a sucker, you know that? You're sweet ... awfully sweet, but you're a sucker just the same."

He agreed.

"And remember this—*you* did not blackmail anybody. I heard the whole row from the terrace. Hell, they must have been able to hear you all over the lake, the way you were screaming. But *you* did not blackmail anybody. You made those pictures in good faith. Just remember that and quit flogging yourself."

"That doesn't help much."

"You'd be surprised. It'll help a lot, later on. And now get up. We're getting out of here, you and I."

"What do you mean? getting out of here."

"Just what I said. If you're going to New York to get set up you might just as well go now. And I'm going with you. I've had a bellyful, too."

"If you think I'm going to New York to start a studio with her money—"

"That's *exactly* what I think. You've earned your chance, now. Take the dough and get started. The sooner you are out from under her the better off you'll be."

"But … what kind of money is it?"

"It's money. Just money. All money looks alike. Don't be so damned squeamish …"

"I won't touch it."

"All right. Then I'll help you."

"Why should you?"

"One—because I like you."

"The hell with that!" He sat up abruptly. "Too many women have told me that during the past ten days and what has it gotten me?"

"Okay. Drop that reason. Two—because I *need* you. You're the reason I have just hit the big time. I need you like crazy and I'm perfectly willing to invest in you as long as you will keep me going. Is that clear?"

"It's clear. I don't like it, but it *is* clear."

"I open next Saturday night. I've got to get back to town. Now is as good a time to go as any. Okay?"

"Okay," he said. "Let me get my stuff together."

When she got to her room, Nell was sitting on the bed, waiting.

"He wouldn't take any of your money," Tony said.

Nell said, "I've got to get him out of here before Matta comes back with the cash. I've got to get him started in that studio so I'll have him where I can get at him."

"Don't worry. I've fixed that. I told him that *I* would stake him, because I need him so badly in my—ah—*career.*" She laughed.

"Did he fall for it?"

"Sure. Like a ton of bricks."

"Good, how much do you want?"

"How about ten thousand to begin with?"

"I'll go and write you a check." Nell left the room.

Tony Ramova set about packing. She was singing a little song.

BOOK TWO—THE ASHES

CHAPTER SEVEN

The yellow safe-light in the darkroom began to blur before Pat's eyes. Without looking, he reached a hand behind him for the bottle of Scotch on the counter. His other hand continued twirling the knob on the enlarger. He couldn't get the picture into focus and he cursed it furiously. His hand found the bottle and lifted it. It dangled from his fingers, empty.

He straightened up irritably and snapped off the enlarger lamp, then went to the door and opened it. Although the light in the huge studio was dim it almost blinded him, and for a moment he stood there blinking his eyes. One hand supported him against the door frame. When he could see he went unsteadily across the large room to a door in the opposite wall. He opened it and stepped through into the living room.

Compared to the studio it was a small room, although its measurements by any ordinary standards were quite large. It was garishly furnished in the most modern of modern. Pat had the usual insane feeling that some day he would come into this room and it would be whirling like a merry-go-round. Nothing was restful. From the bumping, grinding pictures of Tony Ramova that lined the walls—huge enlargements in brilliant color, every one taken in a moment of violent motion—to the mobiles that hung from the ceiling, the chairs that looked like hairy spiders, the lamps that brought a voodoo witchdoctor's feverish imagination to mind, the whole room seemed to be in a perpetually writhing, entangled movement that tugged and strained at the nerves and hammered relentlessly at the brain.

Pat closed his eyes for a moment. This was a room for Tony. This was Tony's room. Her taste. Her environment, where she received her friends, if you could call them that, the strange keyed-up hopheads that hung around the outskirts of her stellar aureole. This was Tony's idea of a good old-fashioned parlor.

A shudder ran over him and he crossed the battlefield of modern furniture to the little bamboo bar by the kitchen door. From the cabinet under the bar, he extracted a fresh bottle. He uncorked it and took a deep swig without bothering with the more genteel services of a glass.

He wanted ice cubes. Still looking with horrified fascination at the room in which he was forced to do his drinking, he backed through the swinging door to the kitchen. He groped for the light-switch and flicked on the neon tubing in the ceiling. He closed his eyes to the eerie pause of darkness after the switch was thrown, the frighteningly human hesitation of the tubes as they flickered tentatively, one by one. He opened his eyes only when he could make out the glow of the fully lighted fixtures through his shut eyelids. Then he turned around.

The kitchen looked like the backlot of a zoo. Tony was a cat fancier. Not to the extent that she would let the hapless beasts into the apartment proper where they might soil her expensive "furniture," but nevertheless, to the extent that she kept five or six of them at the same time. This particular batch was Siamese, and Pat felt like Daniel in the lions' den as he looked about at the six pairs of evil eyes that glinted at him from every section of the filthy room. Tony kept a couple of sandboxes for them, but as usual she had forgotten to change the sand in them.

Gingerly he made his way to the refrigerator, opened the door and extracted a few cubes from the tray below the freezing unit. The minute he turned his back on the cats, he seemed to hear little velvety, shuffling noises all about him. He got the dreadful feeling that they were closing in on him, and leaving the icebox door open, he whirled about.

But the cats were not about to leap. They were still crouched in their various corners. He breathed a sigh of relief and pushed the refrigerator door shut with the heel of his hand. Then he beat a hasty retreat to the screaming, but less dangerous living room. He got a large tumbler from under the bar, dumped the ice cubes in it and filled it to the brim with straight Scotch. Then, carefully selecting a spindly chair that looked as if it might possibly be able to support him, he sat down, shutting his eyes to the glare of the room. He started sucking on his drink, like a hurt child with a bottle.

He made a wry face. It seemed to him that the ice cubes tasted of the cats and their stink in the kitchen.

The phone rang. He leaned forward slowly, placed his glass on the carpet and went to pick up the instrument. A high-pitched dandified voice came over the wire—"I wish to speak to Miss Ramova."

"She's not here."

"Who is this talking?"

Pat's face twisted into an ugly grin. "This is the sucker."

"Who?"

"I said, this is the butler."

"Very well. You may tell Miss Ramova that Pietro Tonelli called."

Pat bowed ironically to the phone. "I am deeply grateful."

"What?"

"I said, thank you."

There was the usual abrupt click at the other end of the wire as Tonelli hung up. Pat replaced the instrument and returned to his drink.

He thought abstractedly that he would like to get a look at this Tonelli some time. The man—if you could call him that— called up almost every day, and generally when he called Tony would be out all night after her work.

In other words, Pat thought drily, she's out almost *every* night.

He took a deep drag on the drink and lay back in the chair, staring at the ceiling. For the five-thousandth time in the last week his career of the past three months flashed through his mind.

It had looked so good. With a twinge of self-pity, which he recognized as shameful under the circumstances, he thought briefly of the double price he had paid for that career. Janey, who had completely disappeared—and an honest, decent, self-respecting life. He shrugged the pity off. What the hell did it matter if he *did* pity himself? Where there was no self-respect there was no pride, no honor, no decency.

And there was no self-respect at all.

It *had* looked good for six weeks or so. He and Tony had moved into the studio apartment just off Washington Square on lower Fifth Avenue. For a short while he had balked at the money she was spending on him—clothes, tons of the very latest photographic equipment, big parties so that he could meet her friends. But she had only laughed at him and gone right on spending. Finally he had succumbed and settled back comfortably into the role of a gigolo. He began to enjoy spending her money.

In return he made dozens of pictures of her—clothed, dancing, stripping, nude, in every conceivable position and light. They were extremely successful pictures and within a very short time, almost overnight, in fact, the beautiful redhead was the talk of the city nightclub circuit and the bistros were vying for her services. Too, many of Tony's friends came to him for pictures, and as he grew rapidly accustomed to the unadorned female form, he was building a reputation for being the hottest thing around in the field.

Although he and Tony lived together—and slept together when Tony was not otherwise engaged—it was only a very short while before Pat, horrified at her mode of life into which he was being dragged, could think of only one thing. To escape from the very trap which he had helped to set for himself. As he became engrossed in his work and as his success grew, he saw more and more clearly just what kind of a mess he had gotten himself into. More than anything in the world he wanted to pay his debt to Tony and escape, to continue without her.

Although he knew the signed confession still rested in Nell Hamsun's safe, he had neither seen nor heard anything of her since leaving the lodge. Gradually the threat of her was fading into nothingness. He felt that if she had not pursued him yet, she never would. Now if he could just pay back Tony and extricate himself from the pesthole in which he lived he could go ahead, and although the mark of his past stupidity would always be upon him he could perhaps atone for it when he was working on his own.

He wanted nothing more than to get out of Tony's life.

He remembered one night in particular. It had occurred about a week or ten days after they had moved into the studio. Pat had been working like a fiend, his back sore with the strain of camera and darkroom work. He had gone to a late movie in order to relax.

When he stepped from the elevator on his return, he heard the laughter, the singing, the shouting and the hooting from the apartment long before he reached the door.

Tony came rushing toward him the minute he entered the room. "Here's my boy!" she shouted. "Here's my own special chicken-pie! Come in. Come in. Join the festivities."

Pat had quit drinking almost entirely and the drink she shoved into his hand was practically straight whiskey. He took a deep slug of it and felt it burning its vicious way through his innards.

From that moment on things went completely mad. He never did find out the names of any of the people involved and it was just as well. He felt he ought to catch up with the fun so he quickly downed a couple of stiff drinks. Through the resulting haze he got a startling revelation of the life of Tony Ramova.

A very young boy, wearing a yellow silk scarf about his neck, eyebrows plucked, cheeks delicately rouged, came and sat at his feet. He placed a soft white hand on Pat's knee. "Honey," he said, "I've seen some of the pictures you've made of Tony. They're absolutely divine! But absolutely. Won't you please take some of me?"

Pat tried to be polite. "Maybe I will," he said, wanting to jerk his knee away from the other's touch. "What kind of pictures?"

"The same kind, darling. Oh, please, I'd be so thrilled."

"The same kind?"

"Yes, darling. Nudes. You'd be surprised. I'm really quite attractive."

Pat could only stare at him.

The boy stood up. "Kids!" he yelled. "Kids! Tony's photographer doesn't believe I would make good nudes."

There were squeals from all sides. "You'd be just lovely!" "Why, ducky, you'd be the prettiest thing ever!" "Exquisite! Exquisite!"

Pat shrugged and buried his face in his glass. When he looked up, the boy was in the process of stripping in the middle of the floor, but before he could finish, his "date" had hurled himself at him—cursing him and showering him with abuse—and dragged him out of the limelight.

The party roared on. Eventually came the chant which Pat was to hear on innumerable occasions afterwards.

"Tony! Tony! Take it off! Take it off!"

The redhead stood up and went to the center of the floor. Two of the mannishly dressed girls—beautiful girls, Pat thought with a sense of loss—went about the room turning off lamps until only the middle was illuminated.

Tony stood straight and unashamed. "Who's going to help me?" she asked.

"I!" "I!" "I!" came the cry from all directions. "We'll shoot for it," said one of the girls. She stepped out into the light and knelt down by Tony's feet. From her jacket pocket she produced a pair of dice. Two other women joined her on the floor and the dice rolled. A tall, muscular blonde who looked like an Amazon won. She rose with an expression of self-satisfaction and the others faded back to their friends in the semidarkness around the outskirts.

Pat wanted to stop the proceedings. Had it been anyone else but Tony, he might have. But he knew Tony was different. During their short life together, she had already demonstrated a great deal of imagination in her relations with him. Besides, for one thing, she was not his wife. For another thing, he really did not care very much what she did. He certainly did not love her, so her life and what she did with it was no concern of his.

Not only that, but a certain thrill seemed to be suffusing the room. It was beginning to tell on him and he *wanted* the performance to go on.

Someone started the record player and Tony began to sway very gently. The tall woman by her side stepped back in order to give her more room, and Tony's dance began.

For once in her life, the redhead was dressed very simply, in a lovely black cocktail frock, sheer stockings and excessively high heels which forced her calves into full tautness and bent her knees slightly forward, thus throwing her thighs into a prominent curve.

Pat watched her face as she went into her dance. She had been drinking, but it was as if the alcohol simply evaporated from her skin now. She seemed completely steady on her feet and her eyes were clear and shining. In fact, Pat was startled by the clarity of her face. It seemed transfixed, like a little girl's—innocent, devoid of guile, happy beyond description. He remembered the way in which she had almost hugged herself with self-pleasure the time he had made the very first pictures of her by the pool up in the mountains, and he realized that he was seeing Tony—for the first time actually—in her real element. She was delirious with pleasure at the opportunity to display her beauty. What disturbed him most was that she appeared to prefer to display it before these women rather than under more normal circumstances.

He could not take his eyes off her as she glided gracefully across the floor. What she was doing was, of course, not a real dance at all. It was more of a walk, designed to show off her lovely figure. It was the ancient stripper's strut and he saw her as the end product of a venerable heritage that went far, far back in American history, clear back to Little Egypt.

He saw something else too, for Pat, though young, was no fool. He saw the story of our times written in Tony's act. He saw the long downhill slide, as though from level to level, down into the inferno.

Born into his very bones and nourished by his reading as a boy was the steel of the pioneer. And alloyed into the steel was the deep-seated sense of freedom, of individuality, of self-reliance, that plowed the prairies and built the cabins, that raised the cattle and formed a nation out of nothing. And tinging that hardened steel was the translucent blue of lustiness, of free men whooping it up on Saturday night. The clear blue tinge of healthy lustiness in which excesses are innocent, because men are innocent. The healthy, roaring, rip-snorting, anything-goes lustiness that today has been watered down to the pale baby-blue of goody-goody "wholesomeness." Bring the kiddies, for we are *nice*. We are clean-cut, Cub-Scout Americans. But we are rotten at the core, for the healthy lustiness that bore fruit in the uninhibited gyrations of Little Egypt has been depraved into the shamefaced, sneaky, tail-between-the-legs and glance-over-the-shoulder crawl of the pale and dirty-minded little man who today creeps blushing but eagerly trembling into the back tents of our carnivals and the darkness of our burlesque theatres.

And Tony was the epitome of today's wanton woman, who teases and toys, whose depravity drips from her pores, because the healthy lustiness is gone and left is only the shame, the embarrassment.

Pat looked about him around the edges of the room. From every corner stared glittering eyes. Women's eyes. Trembling fingers twitched aimlessly in tight-closed laps. He could hear their shuddering lungs. He could almost feel the jerky expulsions of their fetid breaths. Women in men's clothing...the new-minted Lotharios of the machine age.

The jungle-beat of the screeching record pounded at his temples as Tony began to strip. She bent forward and her hands touched her knees. Then they started upward, carrying the hem of the dress with them. They slid along her thighs until white flesh gleamed above stocking tops. They slid along the flesh. When they reached her loins, they dropped the dress, but continued upward, sliding flatly across her belly and up until they rested lasciviously under her full breasts. They lifted the breasts ever so slightly, then they slid on, curving over the softness until they reached her throat. There they rested for an instant before being flung violently apart.

The living, fluttering, violating hands went to her side and the little hiss of a zipper was heard. She ripped the dress over her head.

In her slip now, she was trembling with ecstasy, shivering and shimmying like a primitive priestess dancing over the boiling cauldron. Her quivering fingers caught the top of the slip and tore it straight down. It hung open like a kimono and she moved backward toward the huge blonde who stood transfixed on the sidelines. She held her arms out behind her and the woman lifted the slip from her shoulders. Tony reached her arms above her head and arched back. The woman caught her about the waist before she fell and pulled her roughly against her.

The dancer tore herself loose and leaped forward onto the middle of the floor once more. Dressed now only in a black net brassiere, black net panties through which her white flesh gleamed, and a little garterbelt which held up the long, sheer stockings, her body threw itself into a series of wild gyrations that seemed to start at the floor and spin their way over her flesh until they flung themselves free at the top of her head.

Pat suddenly noticed that several of the women were standing, where before they had been sitting. They were leaning forward tensely, their evil eyes glittering.

And Tony offered herself up to them, fantastic delirium written in every part of her face and body. Again she backed toward the tall blonde, who reached great, clawlike hands forward and unsnapped the brassiere between the girl's shoulderblades. It fell away in her hand and Tony's breasts swung free—taut and quivering with excitement. Swiftly she crushed them under her hands. She flung herself on the floor and rolled maniacally on the carpet, little gasps escaping her lips.

Her fingers plucked at the elastic of the black panties. Slowly she rolled them down, little by little. She lifted her knees and slid the panties clear of her legs. One of the women stooped and picked them up. She stood crushing the fragile material between her fingers, while she watched.

The white body on the floor rolled restlessly. Pat saw that little flecks of blood were appearing at the corners of Tony's mouth where she had bitten her lips. Her eyes were closed and her face was gradually becoming more and more flushed.

Pat staggered to his feet. He fled out of the room. He ran through the studio and into the darkroom. He slammed the door and flung himself into a corner of the coal-black cell. There he crouched on the floor, whimpering like an idiot, his mind a mad kaleidoscope...

After that night he avoided her parties. They were too strong for his blood. Tony resented it, but when he saw one of her orgies building up, he would go into their bedroom and lock the door. Then he would lie on the bed, thrashing and turning, listening to the bacchanalian sounds from the living room, desperately trying to pass into the oblivion of sleep.

More and more he isolated himself. More and more he worked with other models, for other performers, and more and more Tony resented it.

The time came when he was completely independent of her. He had hired a darkroom assistant and a receptionist and even greater numbers of his pictures appeared on the billboards in front of the night spots of the city. More and more performers sang his praises.

And then one day he owed Tony only one thousand dollars and he saw his way clear to pay that off within a week. He began to look about for new quarters. He began thinking about branching out into other fields of photography. The bright little light of success seemed to be shining now down at the end of the dark corridor, the entire length of which he had almost traveled.

Then Tony struck.

As long as he lived, he would never be sure exactly why. He thought it might be jealousy, because he was helping others climb the steps up which he had shown her the way. But it did not seem quite logical.

Suddenly his appointments were canceled by the people who, only the day before, had clamored for them. Suddenly he was alone in the big studio. Suddenly he no longer needed a darkroom assistant. Suddenly a receptionist was a useless luxury.

Then he was alone.

It took exactly two weeks.

At first he did not understand what had happened. Then gradually the truth dawned upon him and he confronted Tony with it.

She only laughed. "You won't go hungry," she said. "You don't need them. All you need to do is to work for me. *Me,* do you hear? You and I, we are a team."

A team! What kind of a team?

He hated her. How he hated her after that. All he could see was that in her jealousy, in her love of herself, she had destroyed him. She had plunged the little light at the end of the hall into Stygian blackness...

Pat dragged himself from the spidery chair, and picking up the bottle, carried it gingerly out of the living room into the studio. He flicked a switch by the door and the huge room was suddenly flooded with light. He looked around it with fondness. This was his room. This was his haven and his heaven.

He crossed the floor to the darkroom door. He went inside and turned on the overhead light. As dark rooms go, it was a beauty. Painted a lovely dark green, it was long and narrow. A thin aisle ran between chest-high counters the length of the room, and everything was handily within reach.

He went down to the very end of the counter and opened a drawer. From the depths of piles of negatives he extracted four or five. He held them up to the light and grunted with satisfaction. These were the ones. He could create havoc with these. And he intended to.

He turned the light on under the glass plate in the retoucher, fastened one of the negatives in place and went to work.

It was six o'clock in the morning when Tony Ramova got home. For once she was alone. Dead tired, she dragged herself from the elevator toward the door to the apartment. An expensive stole of matched mink was slung over her arm and hung to the floor. The clean-cut beauty of her black dress was marred by the stains of a couple of spilled drinks. Her hair was mussed and she was a little drunk.

Tony was in the process of hating herself. Not for anything she had done, but because she had permitted her person to become unattractive. Although there were no mirrors about she knew only too well how she looked. She felt about her own body and appearance very much the way a husband would feel about the appearance of his wife. She was cursing herself for looking sloppy, exactly the same way a husband might berate his wife for not looking her best. Tony's relationship with her own body was peculiar, to say the least.

When she got to the door she stopped and wearily leaned her head against it before putting her key in the lock.

That was when she heard the insane laughter from inside.

She straightened up and listened. The laughter rolled and soared and bounced from the walls of the apartment. It penetrated the front door in fits and starts. One second, she could hardly hear it as the laughter gasped for breath, then it roared at her through the thin wooden panel.

She put her key in the lock and opened the door.

At first she saw nothing out of place except Pat, who was sitting in a chair in the middle of the floor, his sides shaking with insane laughter. She closed the door softly behind her and went closer to him, staring in wide-eyed wonder.

Then she saw what he had done, and a ghastly, cold wave of terror ran through her. Pat had removed every one of the gorgeous pictures of her which had adorned the living-room walls. In frozen horror, she regarded the replacements he had put up in their place.

The walls were now lined with fiendishly clever, unbelievably cruel distortions, partly of the same pictures and partly of other negatives which he had taken from his enormous file on her.

All the color was gone and they were all in black and white. Through retouching, he had turned a dozen images of her into devilish caricatures.

There was no mistaking Tony Ramova, but it was a Tony Ramova who stared from horribly twisted, deep-eyed faces, from hunchbacked bodies, from naked figures covered with the festering sores of leprosy, from poses twisted into grotesque and painfully ugly distortions of her dances.

She froze and stood as if she were the salt statue of Lot's wife. Then gradually her mouth opened grotesquely and a dreadful, snarling scream issued from her throat. She clasped her arms about her, as if every one of the pictures had been etched on her own person, and she tried frantically to hide the violation of the very beauty she adored.

If Pat had spent the rest of his life dreaming up some fiendish meanness to do to Tony, he could not have thought of a better one.

For Tony loved her body beyond the love of man. She loved it so much that at times she could wake up in the middle of the night, bathed in the sweat of a recurrent nightmare … her lovely body, torn and mutilated by any one of a number of accidents which came to her again and again.

Now, she felt as a physical pain the mutilation of her pictures—her pictures which had hung upon these temple walls as idols to be worshiped by herself. It was as if Pat had desecrated the very altar of a church.

Screaming incoherent curses at the crazily laughing man in the chair, she caught up a heavy glass ashtray that sat on the little table beside her and hurled it with all her strength at him.

She saw his scalp split and she saw the blood come. She watched with white, set face as he slumped forward and the laughter slowly died.

When the neighbors, who upon hearing her piercing scream had fetched the manager with his duplicate key, came into the apartment a few moments later, they found her weeping hysterically. She was crouched in the center of the carpet, her arms wrapped about her head to shut out the dozen mocking, leering images that hung on the wall.

CHAPTER EIGHT

As the haze slowly cleared Pat groaned and turned over on the creaking bed. The blanket smelled of sweat and the staleness sent a wave of nausea from the pit of his stomach into his throat. He retched and burrowed his face into the moist, lumpy pillow.

Someone was at the door. He heard the knock, but tried desperately to escape from the sound. It hammered at the old wound in his head and throbbed in his temples. The knock came again and the door rattled on its hinges. He raised himself on one elbow and reached for the bottle that stood on the chair beside the bed. He held it to his lips and drained the last few drops from its bottom.

He tried to sit up while the knocking continued, but the effort was too much for him and he fell back on the bed again. Let 'em knock. It was probably Meyer again for the rent. Well, he didn't have the rent and to hell with Meyer.

Painfully his bloodshot eyes circled the cell in which he lived. Peeling wallpaper, cracked ceiling, broken window-pane, rickety bureau, chair and stinking bed. He thought wryly, just like a story about a down-and-outer. All the props. All of them, even to the empty bottle on the broken chair.

He turned his head toward the wall and closed his aching eyes.

The knocking came again, even more insistent this time, but Pat did not move. Not even when he heard Janey's voice, calling his name again and again…

Janey lowered her closed fist and gave up knocking. She knew that Pat was in there. She knew that he was sick of body and sick of mind. She wanted so badly to help him.

Slowly and hesitantly she raised her arm again, but before she had knocked once more she lowered it and turned away from the peeling door. As she turned, she saw a door to the opposite apartment quickly closing. She took a step toward it, but then she gave that up, too.

Step by step, she began to descend the creaking stairs, her head bowed, tears in her eyes.

It had taken her almost two months to find Pat. Gradually, she had followed his trail all over the city—from studio to apartment, from apartment to rented room, from rented room to this filthy tenement. She had followed the descent of his fortunes as she followed the deterioration of his living quarters. She found the photographic stores that had bought his equipment, piece by piece. She discovered the secondhand stores that had bought his clothes, garment by garment. She had been in the pawnshop which had lent him fifteen dollars on his ultimate property, the camera. She had redeemed the camera, for it was Pat's means of making a living and she knew that without it there was only one way he could go. She was carrying it with her now, hanging from her loose and tired arm.

But when she had found Pat himself he had not wanted to open his door to her. She did not know what to do. She could not give up. She could not live, knowing that the man she loved above all others—no matter what he had done—was on the bottom rung of the ladder about to step off into space.

She knew she would be back. She would be back again and again and again and some day he would *have* to open the door.

She left the building and stepped out into the teeming street. The sidewalk traffic swallowed her up. She did not see the cynical eyes that watched her leave, the eyes that were hard as flint.

The eyes of her mother ...

Nell Hamsun saw her daughter leave the building. She stepped out of the doorway where she had been waiting and crossed the busy street, dodging in and out among the rushing cars and trucks.

Outside the front door she hesitated for an instant, then opened the door and went in. She began the long climb up the stairs with a little smile on her face.

When she got to his door, she knocked. There was no answer and she knocked again. When she still received no answer, she rummaged in her purse and extracted a key. She unlocked the door and entered the room.

Pat was lying on the dirty, rumpled bed. He was staring straight at her, but it was as if he did not see her. Finally he turned his head away and muttered, "How'd you get in here?"

Nell smiled as you would smile at a child. "I had a little talk with your landlord before coming here. I paid your rent. Mr. Meyer was quite co-operative. It occurred to me that you just might not open the door to me. So I thought I'd take precautions."

"Well, you're in. So sit down, if you can find a place to sit."

Nell looked about the filthy room and shuddered. "What a mess," she murmured.

"Not the same as a Park Avenue apartment, is it?" he said without turning his head.

"No, it isn't. Oh, well, let's get it cleaned up." She removed her fur coat and like any housewife, went about the room, straightening, tucking his dirty clothes into drawers to get them out of the way. She found an old rag stuck behind the bureau and gave the room a good dusting. Little by little she made the cell look quite respectable.

"Don't look so startled," she said quietly. "Even I had to keep house once."

"I wonder what you were like then."

"Young and pretty. That's what I was like. And a damned good wife." Then she added bitterly, "Too damned good for that schmoe."

"Tsk, tsk, tsk," he sneered, "bitterness does not go well with so smart a frock. Neither does the dusting, for that matter."

She came to the bed. "Now get up and let me clean up the mess you're lying in."

"I couldn't get up if I tried."

"Oh, nonsense, of course you can. I've dealt with drunks before. In fact, I was married to one until I tossed him out. Every one of you can get up if you feel like it."

"I don't feel like it."

She grinned suddenly. "I'll *make* you feel like it." She reached into the voluminousness of her shoulder bag and brought out a bottle of Scotch.

"Gimme that!" he cried and held out both hands.

"Come and get it," she said and placed it on the window sill.

Pat was out of bed faster than he might have thought it possible. He stumbled across the room and caught the bottle in both hands. With trembling fingers he ripped the cap off and turned it to his lips. He drank the stuff as though it were water.

Nell watched him, partly in amusement, as if he were a funny monkey in the zoo guzzling a soda-pop, and partly with disgust. He was not a pretty sight. Then she turned to making the bed, her nose wrinkled as the staleness rose like fumes from the sheets.

When she was through, Pat was standing by the window, the almost half-empty bottle dangling from his hand, a happy, contented expression on his face.

"Now I want to talk to you," she said and sat down on the bed.

"Talk away. As long as you don't take the bottle away from me." He turned around and sat on the sill, his back to the window.

His face was in shadow and she recognized that as long as she could not see the ravages of the drinking he still looked handsome and broad-shouldered and powerful. Her old hunger for him stirred a little in her loins and she moved restlessly on the bed. But she pushed it far to the back of her mind and began speaking. "You can't go on like this, Pat"

"Why not?"

She did not answer his direct question. Instead she said, "I looked for you at Tony's place, but it seems that she is not very fond of you any more."

"I'm not very fond of her."

"I can understand that. What I can't understand is how you let her self-centeredness get you down to this extent."

"I don't give a damn about her self-centeredness. She put me out of business. I went from riches to rags in no-time flat. That's a little hard on any guy."

"You're a weakling, Pat. You know that?"

He held out the bottle. "Here, have a drink. You bother me."

"I intend to bother you. I'm not going to let you stay like this."

"Why not? You've had a hand in it yourself."

"I? How?"

"You started me off in this whole mess."

"Oh, come now! You're a big boy, Pat. I couldn't have made you do a thing you didn't want to do yourself."

He turned sulkily away.

She went on. "Anyway, that's neither here nor there. The fact is that I need your services, Pat."

He looked long at her. "Oh, great. Great. Another little set of blackmail pictures?"

"Not exactly, no."

"What is it this time?"

"I want you to make some pictures out in the Midwest."

"What kind of pictures?"

"You'll find out when you get there."

"Nothing doing."

She got up and reached for the bottle. He snatched it out of her reach. She shrugged and started to pick up her coat and bag.

"It doesn't make much difference, anyway. It will soon be gone and then where will you get more?"

He looked slyly at her as she shrugged into her coat. "What if I took your dough and went on out there and then disappeared?"

"You might try it and find out."

"What's in it for me?"

"Two thousand dollars and expenses and I'll help you get your studio set up again. I need you in a studio."

"Why me? Why me, for heaven's sake? The world is lousy with photographers."

"You're good at it and I like you. Besides, I already have you hooked. It would be a lot of trouble to hook another. Not all photographers are as young and stupid as you have been."

"Why not just send somebody with a box Brownie? They make good pictures."

"I don't trust amateurs to make the kind of pictures I need. They have to be clear and detailed and extremely recognizable."

"I told you I won't do it."

Nell was getting impatient. "Now let's stop playing, Pat You've got no choice at all. I hate to remind you of this, but I happen to have in my possession—"

He interrupted her. "I know...a little paper, signed, sealed and delivered by me." He stepped a little closer to her. "Why don't I just kill you and get it over with?"

She did not budge an inch. "Go ahead," she said. "What do you think it will get you?"

He went and sat on the bed, holding the bottle between his knees. "Okay," he said. "When do I go?"

Pat was met at the airport by an exceedingly well-dressed middle-aged gentleman who looked as if he might be the head of an insurance firm. This was exactly what he was. His handsome face was all smiles as he greeted Pat effusively. He helped him carry the brand-new photographic equipment to his waiting car and whirled him away over quiet country roads that led eventually into an exclusive residential district on the outskirts of the little midwestern town. He ran the car up a neat tree-lined drive and in under a portico at the side of the large red-brick house.

They were greeted cordially by a handsome woman who came to the door and ushered them in. Pat discovered that the man's name was Paul Tilton, that he owned a large and prosperous insurance and real-estate business in town, and that the lady was Margaret Tilton, his wife.

Pat was more than a little confused as he sat down to dinner with the gracious Tiltons, enjoying their excellent food and engaging small-talk. He kept asking himself over and over how in the name of heaven could these two fine people tie in with Nell Hamsun?

Nothing was said about the reason for his visit, and more than once, during dinner, was he tempted to bring the conversation to the point that was burning in his mind. He held his tongue, however, and let matters take their course.

He did not have long to wait. After dinner, Mrs. Tilton said, "I know you boys have things to talk about. Why don't you go into the den and I'll bring your coffee and a bottle of something or other in there. Then you can get your business straightened out."

Paul Tilton grinned, took Pat by the arm, and led him into a booklined study just off the living room. One wall of the room was hidden by a large glass case filled to overflowing with golf trophies. On the other walls hung large photographs of Tilton winning one tournament after another, or receiving silver trophies, or smiling engagingly into the camera as he demonstrated his favorite putting position. It was the kind of cozy, luxurious room where a wealthy man might retire of an evening to enjoy the fruits of his full and good life.

Tilton waved Pat to a large leather chair and sat down himself on a deep couch. He waved his hand at the trophies and the pictures of himself and said, half apologetically, "We all have our vices. This is mine. I admit that I am overly fond of myself as a competitive golfer. As a matter of fact, I *am* rather good at the game."

"It certainly looks that way," said Pat.

For a little while they talked aimlessly about sports, a subject about which Pat knew virtually nothing. Then Mrs. Tilton brought the coffee and a tray that held a bottle of bourbon, soda, ice and glasses. She poured the coffee and smilingly withdrew.

Tilton took a sip from his scalding cup. Then he grinned. A very engaging grin it was, too, and Pat saw a fleeting glimpse of the perfect Rotary president, introducing a somewhat difficult subject at the weekly luncheon meeting. "Now," he said quite abruptly. "Business."

Pat waited and Tilton went on. "Did Mrs. Hamsun tell you what she was sending you out here for?"

"She told me she wanted some pictures. She didn't tell me of what."

"Yes—pictures, that's right." Tilton grinned again, but this time the grin was not quite so charming. "Some very special pictures."

"Yes?"

The man stood up and walked across the room until he was standing in front of the brick fireplace. The flames outlined him in red and orange and yellow, and Pat thought of Mephistopheles. But then the image was shattered as the carefully modulated, cultured tones of the voice of a successful businessman went on.

"I expect you can be trusted," said Tilton bluntly. "I don't think Nell would have sent you here otherwise." He waited as if for an answer, but receiving none he went on. "Since that is so, I will tell you the whole story. It is quite simple, actually. We have in this town a rather progressive group of youngsters—some of them in high school, some of them not. In fact three or four of the young ladies in the group are married, although they are only sixteen or seventeen years old. I believe that in New York you would refer to such a group as a 'gang' of teenagers. It is composed of girls entirely and they go in for a little bit of everything—a little larceny, a little mayhem, a little blackmailing. But mostly they go in for liquor and sex. It's a somewhat vicious little bunch, to say the least. However, I am led to understand that in this endless postwar era such a group is not uncommon. This gang is rather remarkable in that a number of its members come from very good families in town. Or is that remarkable? Perhaps it is true of all these gangs. Naturally, their families know nothing of their extracurricular activities, although they are fairly common knowledge about town. Some of the girls are in the group voluntarily and some of them are in it because they think it is a must. Others, although the shenanigans are abhorrent to them, are tagging along because their friends are involved or because they have been threatened into joining or for some other reason of coercion or semi-coercion. Actually the gang is controlled by only two or three girls and the others are led around like sheep. Have you ever heard of such a bunch of young fools?"

"Sure. You find them everywhere these days."

"All right, then. You may wonder how I come into the picture. Well, the answer is quite simple. Nell Hamsun and I used to work together in other places. Using my profits from those deals I moved here and established myself as a respectable businessman. And I may say I have succeeded quite well for a man with as little education as I have."

He made a vague gesture about the room. "However, this sort of living is expensive, and as the creditors have begun to close in on me, I have had to cast about for a way of getting them off my back. It is only a very short step from there to Nell and these teenagers about whom I have known for a couple of years. See? Very simple."

"I see. I am sure you realize that I was asking no questions."

"I know, but I believe in partners being open and aboveboard with each other, don't you?"

"Within reason, yes."

"I understand. You feel that I am beyond reason?"

"I didn't say that."

"No, but you implied it." There was a dangerous glint in Tilton's eyes. Pat waited to see what the man would do, but his face relaxed and he smiled wryly. "I know, I know. I talk too much. Always have. It's been the bane of my existence. Brother, where I could be today if I could only keep my trap shut. The opportunities I have lost. Oh, well, being talkative is a great asset in the insurance and real-estate business. I just wish it was a little more lucrative."

He shrugged and went on. "Anyway, here's the deal. Through go-betweens I have arranged a meeting between you and the leaders of this gang. I told them that just for the thrill of taking them, you want to make some pictures—nudes, of course—of a couple of the girls. It so happens that the two most reluctant members of the organization are also the prettiest—the ... shall we say ... most desirable? The leaders of the group are rather anxious to get them into line, as they have plans for them. Such pictures would be a great aid in their efforts. They are quite enthusiastic about the plan."

Pat stood up. "That's the craziest thing I ever heard," he said. "What the hell do you take me for? You want me to work for a little bunch of juvenile delinquents? What'll that get *you*? Peanuts?"

"You won't be working for *them*. And don't get so excited."

"If I'm not working for them then what *am* I doing?"

"With their enthusiastic co-operation you will take your pictures of the girls. But you will not give them to their leaders. You will give them to my wife and me."

"Your wife?"

"My wife is my little helpmeet in all my endeavors."

"I see. And then?"

"Then your job is finished and you return to New York and rest on your laurels."

"And what about the pictures?"

"They stay here with us."

"What for?"

"That is of no importance to you. All you need worry about is getting them."

"I see. And you think I'm going to do this to a couple of innocent young girls?"

"I imagine you will. Nell said something about—"

"A paper I signed. Thank you for reminding me." Pat swung away furiously. His mind was a seething furnace of anger and frustration. He knew he was hooked. If he did not want to end up in jail as a blackmailer he had no choice. The thought occurred to him that he might just let Nell make use of his "confession" and then drag her down with him. But then he realized that he had absolutely nothing on her in the way of solid proof. And he thought of Janey. No matter how evil Nell was, she was Janey's mother. And not only that, but she was a highly respected lady with a fashionable apartment on Park Avenue. She moved only in the very best of circles. He knew that he would never be able to make anything stick on her.

He shrugged, as he had had to do before since becoming involved in this vicious mess, and murmured, "All right."

Tilton rubbed his palms together. "Good," he said. "Fine! I knew you would co-operate. And don't worry about those girls. They're not exactly what you would call innocent."

Pat would hardly have called it "co-operation," but he said nothing.

"Oh, one thing more," Tilton said. "You understand, of course, that I am a very respected man in this community. Up until now my name has in no way been connected with this little business. It never *will* be connected with it. Is that clear? Any negotiating that has to be done will always be carried out by middlemen. That goes for you too. You will go to the picnic which is being arranged, and that is all."

"Picnic?"

"Yes. I am arranging a wiener roast on one of my properties out in the country."

Pat laughed a little hysterically. "A *weiner roast!*"

"I see your point. Oh, well, it has to be called something. My contacts are arranging for other refreshments too, of course. When the girls are in the right mood you will step in and make the pictures of the two in question. They will be pointed out to you by their leaders."

"Isn't it a little cold for that kind of picture?"

"It can't be helped. That, as the gang-leaders will put it, will be part of the test of good will which these girls must endure in order to remain members of the organization. If the girls are reluctant you will receive a little help. It is all arranged."

"So I see," said Pat drily.

"Now, young fellow, how about a drink? To sort of clinch the bargain, eh?" Tilton went to the door and called his wife. "Margaret, come on in. It's all settled. Come in and join us for a drink."

Mrs. Tilton came in, all smiles, all gracious hostess, and the gathering took on the nightmarish quality again of being just a polite visit among respectable people.

At the end of the evening Tilton drove Pat over back roads to within a block of the town's hotel. He put him out of the car with the admonition to be very careful about being seen around too much. Finally, in parting, he said, "Keep a close watch out of your hotel window on that office window over there across the street. That is one of the windows of my private office. When you see a small potted plant sitting on the sill—this will be within a couple of days—ask the hotel clerk to tell you where the cemetery is and explain to him that you want to make some pictures of the old headstones. Walk out there. It's no more than a quarter of a mile. Bring your equipment with you. Somebody will pick you up there, and after you have made your pictures, will bring you back to the same place. Is that clear?"

"It's clear."

"Okay. Good luck." The car roared off and Pat walked the block to the hotel, carrying his camera and his suitcase. He registered and went up to the front room he had requested. After the bellhop had gone, he went to the window and cautiously parted the curtains. He looked straight across the street at Tilton's office window. He turned back into the room and opened his suitcase. From its depths he extracted a bottle of whiskey. He placed it on the night table. Then he fetched a glass from the bathroom. He filled the glass from the bottle and sat down on the bed.

There he sat in the night, waiting for a small potted plant to appear in a window. He was hurting inside, but the liquor helped …

Two days later, at noon, the plant appeared.

Pat did as he was told. He asked his way to the cemetery and walked out there, a young photographer obviously intent on making some pictures of an interesting old landmark. As he walked along he thought of the past two days spent making pictures around the town, going to the movies and drinking alone in his room. He had made quite an effort to appear inconspicuous, and around him a slightly mysterious aura had grown up. It was rumored about town that he was working for a national magazine about to do a story on the little city. Everyone was very co-operative and in general they had left him alone to go about his business.

The cemetery turned out to be on a very lonely road completely surrounded by woods. It was a perfect place for a rendezvous of this type.

Pat sat down on the crumbling stone-wall and waited. He had been there for better than an hour when a car came tearing along the road. It skidded to a stop and a hand waved at him out of the partly open window. He picked up his camera and gadget-bag and walked over. The door was opened and he slid into the front seat next to the driver.

It was a girl. A small blonde girl, really only a child, dressed in sweater and skirt and bobby-sox. She was wearing a leather windbreaker against the cool air. "Hi," she said.

He said, "Hi," and felt exceedingly uncomfortable as he regarded her. She had a woman's face over a girl's body. The face of a woman, in fact, who had been around.

She said nothing further. Like a maniac she drove over the back country roads, weaving in and out among hedges and woods and fields. Finally, when Pat thought that surely they were approaching the end of the world, she swung into an almost hidden lane that led through a thicket of brambles for something like a quarter of a mile.

They came to a little clearing where several cars were parked and she pulled into a space between two bushes and stopped the car. She sat there a minute, breathing deeply, evidently still tasting the exhilaration of the hurling, rocketing, weaving ride. She was a good driver and it was quite obvious that driving gave her a thrill that carried with it some sort of inner satisfaction for her.

Then she opened her door and stepped out on the ground, motioning for Pat to follow her. He slipped out, still carrying his equipment, and joined her. She nodded up the lane and muttered, "This way."

He followed her as she strode along, her gait very much like a boy's, and after a little while the lane widened out and he began to hear the sounds of girls laughing and shouting to each other. When they came within sight of the picnic they stopped. They were still hidden by bushes which grew between them and the cabin in the center of the little clearing.

The party was going on, both inside and outside the little log house. It appeared to be in full bloom. Several liquor bottles were in evidence on the stoop of the cabin, and there was something in the demeanor and behavior of the girls that appeared almost pathetic to Pat. In spite of the cold winter air the girls had set up a phonograph in one of the windows of the house. Several of them were dancing together on the hard-tamped ground in front of the door. They were dancing unnaturally close, cheek to cheek, body to body. Others sat on the steps, staring straight ahead with glassy eyes and deeply contented faces, lost far off in their alcoholic Eden.

Pat could not take his eyes off the spectacle before him and he gave a violent start when the girl touched his arm. He turned his head and found her grinning at him.

"Like it? Except for the few boys we've brought out for various purposes you're the only man who has ever witnessed one of our parties."

He looked back at the other girls and shuddered as he thought of their families, of their fathers and mothers.

The girl at his side went on. "You can't come any closer. None of the others must know that you are here. I'm going to go in while you wait here. After a while a couple of us will bring the two girls out this way. You let us pass and then follow us at a discreet distance. When we want you we'll let you know."

She left him and ran down the lane toward the house. He watched her as she crossed the clearing and wound up by the front steps. She sat down with a couple of the girls and accepted a cigaret from one of them. Pat wondered how long he was going to have to wait.

It turned out to be quite a while.

As the afternoon wore on and Pat grew colder and colder, the party became more and more frenzied on the part of some of the girls, and more and more trancelike on the part of others. Towards four o'clock several of them were lying on the little porch, heedless of the cold, their eyes staring, wide and unblinking, into the clear blue sky. Only a few were still dancing, and as they now danced Pat saw their hands wandering restlessly over each other's bodies and their mouths meeting in long, avid kisses.

The dances reached a point where he could no longer watch. He turned his back and sat down on a rock, smoking, trembling with the cold and cursing himself for being there at all.

A piercing scream from the cabin brought him to his feet and as he watched he saw a spectacle that would have seemed much more at home in the dense forests of Haiti.

The girl who had screamed leaped from the porch into the center of the dancing group. The other girls gave way and formed a circle, enthusiastically shouting and clapping their hands.

The girl, a slender, dark-haired, pretty little thing, flung her body into horrible contortions, her hips bumping and grinding, little breathless screams bursting from her lips from time to time. The other girls gave her more room and stood back, accompanying her dance with their handclaps. They were obviously in a state of tense expectation.

They did not have long to wait. Her head flung back, her hips working, and her breath heaving laboriously, the dark-haired girl started ripping at her blouse. She jerked it from her shoulders as the spectators roared approval. She continued with the skirt. The last Pat saw of her, she was writhing in the middle of the group, dressed only in her small yellow panties and a thin brassiere.

He missed the rest of her dance, for while the group's attention was riveted on the dancer, four girls came from behind the cabin and walked slowly and cautiously toward the lane where he was hiding. Pat recognized the blonde who had brought him out. With her was another larger girl, who looked a little older than the rest. In front of them walked two uncommonly pretty girls, both obviously quite young, both dark and slender and well dressed. Pat was amazed to see that they were blindfolded and were being guided by the other two.

As they passed his hiding place Pat heard one of them say in a small whimper, "But what are you going to *do* to us?"

The larger girl answered, "You'll find out. You know what the rules are. No questions."

When they were down the lane a little way Pat reluctantly followed them. He had never hated himself as he did at that moment. After a short distance the girls left the road and started cutting through the bushes. Eventually they came out in a small clearing by the banks of a creek. The two leaders stood the girls side by side with their backs toward the creek. There was a steep cliff on the other side that formed a perfect backdrop for the pictures.

The older girl commanded gruffly, "Take off your clothes."

The two victims stood transfixed.

"Off with them—or do you want Sally and me to take 'em off you?"

"But ... but why?" The smaller of the two was crying. "Why?"

"Look. You know the rules, I said. No questions."

The taller of the two bit her lips below the blindfold. "I won't do it."

"Is that a fact? The two of you have been hanging around for thrills now for three weeks. We've let you in on everything and you've done nothing in return. Now let's see you prove yourselves. And you'd better do it voluntarily. Any other way would be more than somewhat uncomfortable for you."

"But what are you going to do to us?"

"Take 'em off and find out."

"Please, please—don't make us do it."

The older girl walked over to the smaller of the two and slapped her viciously across the cheek. "Get going," she said.

Trembling, the two girls began to remove their clothes.

The blonde, Sally, backed up until she was standing just before the bush where Pat was concealed. She said softly, "Come out of there quietly. When I say *now*, take your picture. Is that clear?"

Pat stepped out beside her and got his equipment ready. Both girls were down to their undies now. Both were trembling with fear and cold.

"Hurry it up," said the older leader.

Pat was conscious of Sally's presence beside him. He had finally made his decision. Come hell or high water, no matter what the consequences would be to him, he could not do this to these children. Like him, they had been foolish and had gotten themselves into a situation that rendered them helpless. He was not going to be the one to further their miseries. No matter what "plans" these two girls had for their victims, no matter what intentions Tilton and Nell had for them, they were not going to become possible through pictures made by him. He knew he was cutting his own throat, but it couldn't be helped.

It made him feel a lot better.

He put the film-holder in the back of the camera and stood quietly watching the two girls as they continued undressing.

His heart quickened in his chest as he saw how lovely they both were. They slowly, reluctantly, removed their brassieres and small panties and stood completely revealed—nubile breasts proud, their little dark tips taut with the cold. Slender white legs and small, boyish hips trembled and fluttered in agitated anxiety.

Pat saw that they were still almost children and he was terribly ashamed to be watching them in such a state. He turned away and started to leave the clearing.

Sally hissed in his ear. "Where do you think you're going?"

He said in a clear, cold voice, "If you kids think I'm going to be a party to this, you've got another think coming, you filthy little brats."

The two nude, blindfolded girls cried out when they heard his voice and tried to cover themselves with their hands and arms.

The older girl leaped forward until she was standing directly before them. "Don't move," she threatened. "Don't move, or you'll wish you hadn't!"

Pat continued on his way until he felt the little gun in the small of his back. "Come back," said Sally softly.

"You know damned well you wouldn't dare shoot," he taunted.

"Oh, wouldn't I? Nobody knows you in town. Nobody knows you're out here. You could just disappear, couldn't you? I wouldn't count on my not daring if I were you."

He hesitated. He thought that the girl was probably bluffing. On the other hand she was hardly what you could call a normal child. Then he thought of another way out and turned around. "All right," he said and shrugged.

"That's better. You just stick with us and nobody'll get hurt." The girl talked like a highschooler's idea of a gun-moll, and if the situation had not been so serious, he would have smiled at her act.

The older girl said, "All right, take off your blindfolds."

The pair lifted shaking hands and removed the black pieces of cloth. Wide-eyed with fright and horrible embarrassment, they stood there, staring at Pat and his camera. "What're you going to do?" asked the taller, breaking into tears.

"Quit your sniveling and you'll find out."

Pat tried desperately to think of a way to signal to the girls that they need not worry, that he was not going to do anything that could hurt them, but he was being watched too closely by Sally.

"Okay, Jeannie," said Sally quietly. "Everything is under control."

Jeannie turned toward the two nude girls again and said, "All right, now. Hold hands and just stand there beside each other. Stop bawling, d'you hear. Look a little pleasant. Look like you enjoy it."

The two girls cried harder and Jeannie took a step closer. The two sniffled and choked back their tears. They clutched hands and stood there trembling with the cold and with their fear, a ghastly grimace representing a smile on their faces.

"Now go ahead and shoot," said Sally.

Pat raised the camera without pulling the slide from the film-holder. That way he could go through all the motions of taking the picture, even snapping the shutter, but because it was covered by the slide, the film would remain blank.

He set the lens aperture and the time and cocked the shutter. He raised the instrument to his face and sighted through the range-finder. He set the focus and snapped the shutter.

Then came Sally's dry voice. "Now try one with the slide pulled out, why don't you?"

He had not fooled her. He started to lower the camera, but the gun poked him gently in the ribs. He pulled the slide.

As he took the picture, he told himself that this was one set of negatives which would never reach any darkroom. As soon as he was dropped off at the cemetery, he would pull the slides again and expose the film to daylight. That should take care of them.

As he was taking the picture, the blonde girl at his side said, "What's with you? We were told that you *wanted* to make some pictures like these."

"I've changed my mind."

"It's too late for you to change it now, brother. Conceivably we could get a box camera and make some ourselves some other day. Conceivably, that is. It might be a little difficult, though, to get these chickens to come and pose for us again, don't you think? And we're not very addicted to using force."

He glanced down at the gun. "What do you call that?"

"That's different. You're nobody around here. But nobody at all."

Jeannie told the girls, "Now embrace each other. Face toward each other and put your arms around each other, real affectionate-like. You know what I mean. Real cozy and close together. Both of you turn your heads this way."

The girls did as they were told, their spirits broken. But both turned their heads away. Jeannie's fist fell with a smack on the naked hip of the smaller girl. She cried out and both girls turned their faces toward the camera this time.

"Remember to remove the slide now, friend," said Sally sweetly. Pat shot the picture. He had a way out, he knew, so there was no sense in dragging the ordeal out any longer than necessary for the two victims.

While the two nude girls grew colder and colder and finally began to cough, he shot picture after picture of them singly and together and gradually the poses grew uglier and uglier.

Finally the two leaders called a halt and allowed the weeping, terrified, trembling girls to put their clothes back on. While they were dressing, Sally marched Pat back to the car, walking behind him all the way, the little gun in her hand.

Before she got in the car, she took his camera and gadget-bag containing the exposed film and locked them in the trunk. Then she got in the front seat and motioned him in beside her. The gun was in her left hand on the steering wheel.

She turned the car around and they hurtled down the lane again, this time in the opposite direction.

As Sally drove, she said, "I don't get you. The information we had was that just for the kicks you wanted to make some pictures. If we had had any idea that you were going to get cold feet you'd never have gotten anywhere near the place. Now you've made everything so damned complicated."

He said, "What did you want those pictures for?"

"What do you mean, *did?* We still do."

"All right. What do you want them for?"

"Oh, we got plans for those chicks. We just need the pictures for a little persuasion. Without the persuasion they might not want to co-operate."

"Co-operate in what?"

"Oh, this and that with the gang. Don't be so nosy."

They drove back a different way from the one they had come. After several miles Sally pulled up at a little house by the roadside.

She turned off the ignition and pocketed the key. Carrying the gun carefully, she stepped out of the car and said, "You wait here a minute. I'll be right back." She went into the house, which appeared to be deserted. Pat got out and walked a little closer. He could hear her talking inside, but it was not possible for him to make out what she was saying or to whom she was talking.

Before he found a way of getting still closer, since it was still broad daylight, she came out again. She laughed when she saw him standing in the middle of the yard. "What's the matter?" she asked. "Getting nosy again?"

He took a couple of quick steps toward her, but she backed away and raised the gun. "Don't be funny," she said.

He felt completely ridiculous, being the unwilling captive of a teenage girl with a gun she probably wouldn't have the nerve to use. On the other hand, he couldn't be sure, and since he still had the comforting knowledge that he ruin the film before it ever got to the darkroom, he shrugged and went back toward the car.

They got in again and she resumed her wild driving.

Just as it was getting dark, they came to the spot where she had picked him up. She stopped the car and they both got out. Sally unlocked the trunk and gestured for him to remove his equipment. He felt quite cheerful as he held it again in his hands. Then, with a wave of her hand and a "So long, sucker," she jumped back in the car and roared off.

Pat watched her tail lights disappear and smiled to himself. This was one dirty job in which he had gotten involved that he could fix before it got any worse. Let Nell throw him to the wolves. To hell with her. He'd had enough. More than enough. He would rather be able to live with himself in jail than not be able to live with himself outside any longer.

He thought of Janey and laughed as he placed the gadget-bag on the stonewall and removed the film-holders from its depths. His laughter stopped abruptly as he felt the hand on his shoulder.

"We'll take those, bub," said a deep voice behind him.

He did not take the time to glance over his shoulder. He ripped the slide from the first one and had started on the second when a terrible rabbit-punch across the back of his neck knocked him to his knees. The film-holders were torn from his fingers as another voice asked, "How many did he ruin?"

"Ah, just one," said the deep voice. Then it continued.

"Don't outsmart yourself, young feller. The girl telephoned and told us you'd got cold feet out there an' she'd had trouble with you. She was afraid you might be planning to do something like this. So we thought we'd just come along an' pick up the pitchers. Real useful girl, that little tomato. Too bad she ain't ever gonna see these pitchers herself. She worked real hard for them."

"Dog eat dog," said the other voice and they both laughed.

Pat tried to turn around to get a look at his tormentors, but a huge fist grabbed him like a vise about the neck. "Just stay the way you are, boy. We like you that way," growled the deep voice.

"Those negatives aren't even developed yet," said Pat.

"Now don't you worry your head none about that. I reckon we can find somebody who can do it for us, since we ain't so sure any more that we can trust you."

He heard their feet shuffling as they backed away from him in the darkening twilight. He started to turn again, but this deep voice said, "You just stay right there, boy, an' you won't get hurt."

Then he heard a car door slam. He sprang up and swung around. From behind the trees where it had been hidden, a black sedan shot out onto the road and roared off. It was almost impossible for Pat to see who was inside, but he thought he caught a glimpse of Mrs. Tilton in the back seat.

He started out on the dreary, defeated walk back to the hotel.

The next day he called at the Tiltons' house, but a maid told him they had left town for an extended trip.

There was nothing for Pat to do but to slink back to New York, not any better off than he had been before, but worse. Much worse.

CHAPTER NINE

Janey saw Pat as he was leaving the glittering glass and chrome building. She ran swiftly across the teeming street to intercept him. "Pat," she cried. "Pat! I've been looking everywhere for you."

He stared at her as though he didn't recognize her, then he turned on his heel and re-entered the building.

She ran along beside him. "Pat," she pleaded, "please, Pat, talk to me. Don't turn your back on me. Please. Please!"

He walked quickly toward the elevator and she gradually realized that people were staring at them, that she was making a spectacle of herself.

"Please, Pat," she begged in a final whisper.

He did not answer. They reached the elevator and he stepped inside, his eyes turned away from her, his face closed.

She stepped back and allowed the elevator door to slide shut. Then she turned and walked blindly from the lobby out into the street. She paid no heed to the curious stares that followed her. Outside, she was soon lost in the crowds…

Pat stopped outside his studio door and for a minute he leaned his head against the door frame. Then he put his key in the lock and entered. He went directly across the tiled floor to a little cabinet against the far wall and extracted a bottle of whiskey. As if he were walking in a dream he went through the narrow door into the kitchen. From the cupboard he got a glass and from the refrigerator he got ice cubes. Then he sat down by the kitchen table and set to work getting drunk.

But the oblivion wouldn't come. He half finished the bottle, then rose, and carrying his glass with him, went into the studio. On a large drafting table that stood next to the darkroom door was a big folder. This he opened. It contained a considerable stack of mounted color prints. He lifted the top one off the pile and held it up in the light.

It was not just an ordinary picture. It was a picture of the city he had come to hate … and to love at the same time. But it was not just an ordinary color picture of the city, either. It was a picture of a tiny fragment of the city, a reflection of half a woman's face, grotesquely twisted as it stared back from a glittering window-pane. Around the face shone the exploding stars of a neon sign from across the street, smeared into abstract streaks by the imperfections in the glass. In any man's language the picture was a masterpiece of abstract color-photography. It was more than that. In the shape of a minute fragment of the whole, it was the perfect portrait of Third Avenue.

And Pat knew it.

But now it did not console him, for now the pain of Janey and of the regrets and the self-hatred was too strong in him. So strong that even the usual anesthesia did not dull it. He set the bottle down carefully and walked away from it, out into the center of the wide floor. He was completely steady on his legs.

He looked about him, hating the beautiful studio that he could now afford. He thought back over the past six months, to the day when he had arrived in New York after his fiasco in the little midwestern town.

He had been beaten. More beaten than he had ever been before, because this time he had really tried to fight Nell Hamsun. But even a thousand miles away from her, he had lost. Lost miserably. And he knew he was licked.

He had taken Nell's money and set up a new studio. He had done everything she wanted from that day on. He had had absolutely no legitimate business. Nell had kept him busy, week after week, making her kind of pictures here and there around the city under strange and dreadful circumstances. Pictures to supply evidence for divorce cases, pictures of drunken, rich young ladies whom he never saw again, pictures of girls in various embarrassing situations—unbelievable, unmentionable pictures—all of them taken in a drunken stupor in which he no longer cared. All of them turned out conscientiously and tossed to Nell contemptuously. All of them paid for in lavish sums which had gone into liquor and equipment for his city abstracts—the only two consolations in his misery, his guilt, and his loneliness.

Three months ago he had started wandering the streets at night. He could no longer sleep. He walked and walked and walked and gradually a feeling came to him—a feeling for the houses and the iron fences and the stoops and the lights and the people of New York. A feeling that could be pictured. Not in ordinary realistic pictures, but in prints that somehow must reflect his nightmare prison.

Then he had started making his pictures—the legs of a sleeping bum reflected in a pool of glittering rainwater; the streak of the subway express as it roared past a station; the glow of cigarets in a darkened doorway where lovers crouched together, their hands shining whitely on each other; the neon constellations of a bar reflected in a glass of foaming beer. All of them pictures of a feeling. Of a feeling for the night city in which his soul was dwelling.

One week ago he had gathered together whatever little shreds of resolution he had left. He had packed up twenty of the prints and sent them to *Skyline Magazine,* one of the biggest picture-weeklies in the country. To date, he had heard nothing and the sense of ultimate failure was so strong in him that it was like a physical pain. And now not even liquor could dull it any longer.

He sat down in a spindly wire chair in the center of the studio, a little lost young man in the huge room. A thin ray of pale moonlight fell upon him from the skylight, like a spotlight on a stage. But the stage was empty of players. The room hummed with silence and the walls did not care that he wept.

It was nearly an hour before Pat raised his head again. He got up and walked slowly to the drafting table. Carefully he closed the folder with the pictures. Then he left the room and the apartment.

Ten minutes later he entered his favorite bar. It was not a fashionable place, but it was a peaceful one, of the variety in which a man can sit in a corner booth for long hours, drinking and being left alone—in which he might hide and have no one knock on the door to his shell. As he entered he headed straight for his booth at the very back of the room. He looked neither right nor left. The bartender shook his head when he saw him, then started reluctantly to pour Scotch over a couple of ice cubes in the bottom of a large tumbler.

A hand reached across the bar and a voice said, 'I'll take it to him."

The bartender looked up at the handsome face of the man who had just entered. His patient expression changed into one of eager respect. "Yes, *sir*," he said and handed the glass over.

Pat did not raise his head when Jacques Fribeaux said, "Here's your drink."

"Just put it down," he murmured wearily.

"Mind if I put myself down, too?"

Pat looked up. For a second he did not recognize the famous actor, then he gestured toward the seat at the other side of the table and said, "Go ahead."

Fribeaux sat down. For quite a while they remained in silence. Finally the actor said, "Look, young fellow, I want to ask a favor of you."

Pat looked up and laughed shortly, "A favor of *me?*"

"I want you to make some shots of me for my agent."

"You'd better get yourself another boy. Or haven't you heard about me."

"I have heard. My agent told me. But it so happens that my agent works for me. I do not work for my agent. I like your pictures."

"I have never taken anything of anybody but women, and you know it. Naked women mostly."

"So what?"

"So what do *you* want? Nudes?"

"Look, boy. I was not born yesterday. I have known Nell a long time. I know all about you. Don't be belligerent."

"And you still want *me?*"

"That was the general idea."

"Why?"

"Don't you want to make them?"

"Pictures of Jacques Fribeaux? Of course I want to make them."

"All right, then."

Pat rose from behind the table. "Look, Mr. Fribeaux, I don't know just what's on your mind. There's nothing I'd rather do than make pictures of you. Not just because it *is* you, but because it might open some doors for me which now are closed and have been closed for a long time. But believe me, it would never work out."

"Suppose you leave that to me."

"Why are you doing this?"

Fribeaux looked off into the haze of the smoky bar. "Why?" He stirred restlessly. "Because once I was in approximately the same position you now are in. Except that it was worse. I was married to the lady."

Pat stared at him in utter amazement. Finally he stammered, "Married? To ... to Nell Hamsun?"

Fribeaux nodded.

"But ... but then ... you're ..."

"Janey's father? Yes, I am."

"But ... but ..." Pat sat back down again. "But for heaven's sake, why don't you tell Janey?"

"Why don't you quit Nell Hamsun and go to work on your own?"

"Because ... because she has certain strings on me that ... oh, I see. You *can't* tell Janey you're her father? Because of certain conditions?"

"That's right. Only mine are a little different from yours. I was very unhappy with Nell. I grew very foolish. I did *many* foolish things, not just one. For instance, I signed very foolish papers in order to get her to agree to a divorce."

"But once—I remember—she said she had *thrown* her husband out."

"A woman has her pride, my boy. I do not doubt but what by now she has convinced herself that this was really so."

"Aren't you ever going to tell Janey?"

"Yes, Pat, I am, and very soon—and to hell with the consequences. I am a rich man now. My career means nothing to me any more. If it destroys my opportunities to act I shall be grateful for the vacation. Yes, my boy, I'm going to tell her. Now will you make some pictures of me? For your own sake? And for Janey's?"

Pat reached across the table and grasped the older man's hand. "Yes, sir. Yes, sir, I will." Then he repeated what the actor had said. "And to hell with the consequences."

He sat for a long time in the booth after the actor had left. He was elated and full of hope. Then he got up, left the bar, and took a cab to Nell's apartment. She greeted him at the door and offered him a drink. He refused and came straight to the point.

"Nell," he said, "I'm going to quit you. Right now."

"Oh?"

"I've been offered an opportunity to make some pictures that may put me back into legitimate business again. I've come to ask you to let me go."

"You mean pictures of Jacques?"

"Yes. How did you know?"

"He told me he was going to ask you."

"And what did you say?"

"I told him to go ahead and try. He doesn't like what I 'have done to you,' as he puts it."

"Well, he asked me and I'm going to do it."

"I doubt it."

"Go ahead and throw me to the wolves. I don't care any more."

"Perhaps you don't care about yourself, but I'd be willing to bet that you *would* care about Jacques."

"What do you mean by that?"

"I mean that if you make these pictures it won't only be you, but him too, that will be thrown to the wolves."

Pat stared at her in disbelief. "Do you really mean that?"

"I do."

"Nell, you are so unbelievably evil that it's almost a miracle."

"I'm not evil, Pat. My war against youth and beauty has only just begun, that's all. I need you. You're my main weapon."

"You wouldn't hesitate to destroy Mr. Fribeaux just because I made some pictures of him?"

"No, I wouldn't."

"Why, Nell? Why am I so almighty important to you? The woods are full of photographers! The woods are full of down-and-out, unscrupulous photographers who'd do anything for a lousy buck! Why *me?*" He was screaming now, the fury and frustration working in his face.

"Simply," said Nell calmly, "because Janey loves you."

"What has that got to do with it?"

"As long as you're working for *me* you'll leave her alone. When she gets married she'll marry money and position." She looked around the luxurious apartment. "I've gone to considerable lengths to get where I am today. Some of the things I've done have not been exactly cricket."

"You can say that again," he muttered.

"But I am here, nevertheless. A respected divorcee of the upper set, purely by virtue of money. Lots of money. And when Janey marries out of this home and this environment, it will be upward and not downward. Is that clear?"

He rose. "It's painfully clear," he muttered.

"Good-bye," she said. "I'll call you when I need you."

Two hours later Pat was drunk. Not roaring drunk, but anesthetically drunk. It had taken close to two bottles, but he had finally succeeded.

Janey, Janey, Janey, he thought, and his need of her was so strong—his need of love, of affection, of security—that he knew he had to have a woman, *any* woman.

He took a cab to an address just off Riverside Drive in the upper reaches of Manhattan. He got out and tipped the knowing driver a ridiculously large amount. He walked steadily—as though behind his own coffin—to the front door and rang the bell. A prim maid opened a little slot in the door, looked him over, recognized him for he had sought solace there before, and opened the door with a pert little curtsy.

"Just send somebody up…anybody," he muttered and stalked past her. He went up a flight of carpeted stairs.

The maid called after him. "The first room to the right, sir."

He went in. It was a sumptuous and very feminine room. He sat heavily on the bed and dropped his head in his hands. When he heard the door open, he raised his head. Then he stood up slowly, his face transfixed, his eyes widening in horror. The girl backed out silently and he stood there staring at the door through which she disappeared.

He was still standing there when she returned. He did not flinch or move as he looked straight into the muzzle of the gun. As from far away, he heard the report as it went off and felt, like the flick of a blowtorch, the searing pain where the bullet burned a deep crease along his side, under his arm. He did not fall, nor did he move, as he watched through a haze the people pouring into the room, taking the gun away from the girl and pinioning her arms when she began the scream and struggle.

"This is what they used your pictures for, you dirty rat!" she shrieked from her scarlet, gaping mouth.

It was the smaller of the two girls he had been forced to photograph that day at the "picnic."

He said through numb lips, "Turn her loose. She didn't do anything. I did. Turn her loose. Nothing has happened. Nothing has happened to me. It has happened to her."

As he left the building, a mad thought ran crazily through his mind. *I never even knew her name. I never even knew her name.*

CHAPTER TEN

The wound on Pat's body was nothing. A little antiseptic. A little plaster. But there was another wound, one that burned deep and straight and true. One that liquor couldn't heal. One that self-hatred couldn't cauterize. One that he must live with. If you could call it living. Yes, *if*.

Three days later he sat in his booth at the bar again. It was the day he had promised Jacques Fribeaux that he would make pictures of him. Pat had not had the courage to call the actor and break the date. To tell him that his nerve had failed him again. That he did not have the strength or the guts to extricate himself from Nell Hamsun's grip. Neither could he make himself tell the actor that he too was in danger if the pictures were taken.

The bartender looked at his young customer, worry written all over his face. He had seen drunks come and go, but never one like this. Three days ago he had drunk steadily, in the ancient and venerable way of a solid lush. Now he just bought one drink and sat and stared into it all night. No alcoholic in the bartender's memory had ever been cured so fast of the habit. He was convinced the boy was sick. Really sick. Nobody in his right mind just sat and stared into a single solitary drink all night without hearing a word spoken to him. Without seeing a thing around him.

The boy was sick.

That was putting it mildly. He was a walking death, that was how sick he was.

Pat hardly noticed when Janey slid into the seat beside him. Nor did he raise his head when she covered his hand with hers.

"Do it," she whispered. "Take his pictures and see what happens."

"You know?"

"I know. I'm glad. He's always been the only one of the people around mother whom I liked."

"He's free of her. Why does he still hang around?"

She smiled. "He loves her."

"What?"

"It is possible to love something abhorrent. People have snakes for pets."

"You ought to know."

"You're not abhorrent, Pat."

He looked at her for a long time, then he stood up. He walked to the telephone booth and called Nell. Her cheery hello made him want to vomit. "I'm going to do it, Nell," he said. "I'm going to make the pictures of your ex-husband." He emphasized the last three words.

"So you know?"

"I know."

"*He* told you?"

"Yes."

"I see. All right, let me tell you this. I'll give the two of you three days to make up your minds. Either you make the pictures and I ruin both of you, or you see the light and keep your noses clean. That's final."

"If you ruin him you'll ruin Janey, too."

"I'll do nothing of the kind. Janey is not to be blamed for the kind of father she had. The divorce is in my name and when I get through with him, the people that matter will see that it was the only thing I could do to save my daughter from an undesirable father. Have you got *that* straight?"

When he did not answer, she hung up in his ear. For a long time he stood in the little booth, staring at the phone on the wall. Then he folded the door back and returned slowly to the table. His shoulders were drooping and his face was a mask, like the face of a badly beaten fighter.

Janey was no longer alone in the booth. A small man with a rosy, cheerful face was sitting beside her. They were in animated conversation when Pat came up.

The little man rose and held out a pudgy hand. "So you're Pat Mulroney," he said and his voice was like a happy laugh. "I'm glad to meet you, boy. You have an eye. Yes, you do, don't you contradict me now, you hear?"

Pat looked at him with his dead eyes and did not know what to make of him.

"Come now, you know *me,* don't you? *Everybody* knows me. I'm Morris." Like an eager child the little man looked at Pat, hoping for and confidently expecting an affirmative answer, but Pat had none.

"Color pictures, h'm? *Skyline Magazine,* h'm? Does that ring a bell?"

Pat still did not answer, so the little man finally gave in. "Oh, darn it, anyway, I'm always hoping *somebody* will know me. You don't know what it's like to be the picture editor of a magazine that specializes in famous faces everybody recognizes at first sight. You don't know what it's like to be a forgotten, anonymous nonentity just because you publish the pictures rather than pose for them. I'm Morris, boy. Bill Morris of *Skyline.*"

"Yes?"

"What's the matter with you, boy? You sent me some pictures. Don't you remember?" He turned to Janey. "Has he been imbibing?"

Janey smiled. "No," she said, "he hasn't. I guess he's just a little stunned."

Pat sat down opposite the other two. He could not take his eyes off Morris. His side ached where the bullet had grazed him and he kept thinking over and over, *Here it is, and it's too late. Too late. Too late.*

Morris was talking. "Now listen, boy. I don't have much time, you know, h'm? I had one hell of a time finding you. But now look. I want you to come to work for me. You've got an eye, you know what I mean? You see things ... not just with your eyes, but with your heart. Those are great pictures. Great, do you hear? Some of the finest photography I've ever seen. I showed them to Jack ... Jack, that's Jack Sowansky, our publisher. You've heard the name, h'm? He said they were great, too. So you're in. I want you to come by my office tomorrow and we'll work out the deal. We'll start by running the abstracts. They're damned good copy, isn't that a fact?"

The whirlwind of words whirled about Pat's ears, but he hardly heard it. *Too late, too late...*

"All right, boy," said Morris, a grin splitting his face from ear to ear. "You're awed by my august presence, h'm? Morris of *Skyline*, h'm? Heck, boy, sometimes I awe myself. That is, until I get home to my wife. She un-awes me in a big hurry, you know what I mean?"

Could this grinning baboon be the editor of a national magazine with the reputation of *Skyline*? But then Morris went on as if he had read Pat's thoughts.

"Don't pay any attention to my clowning, boy," he said. "It's nothing but nerves. Come by my office and see me tomorrow, h'm?"

Pat nodded. He did not actually know he was doing it, but Morris was satisfied with it. He patted him on the shoulder and said, "That's the boy. Sleep on it and don't get excited. There are twenty-seven photographers working for *Skyline*. You'll just be one of the boys. It's nothing to lose sleep over. And confidentially, it's no way to get rich either."

He took effusive leave of Janey, rose and disappeared in the smoke of the bar as if he were really the hobgoblin he seemed to be.

They sat in silence for a long time after he had gone. Finally Janey said timidly, "Pat?"

He looked up at her, his eyes blank and expressionless. She went on. "This *is* what you've been wanting, isn't it?"

He said, "Yes," tonelessly, and let it go at that.

"Then why aren't you happy? Do you want me to go away?"

He reached across the table and caught her hand. He clung to it as though it were a straw to save him from drowning. "No," he said. *"No!"* His voice was like a cry.

She covered his hand with hers. "I want to help you, Pat," she murmured. Then she added, "My father wants to help, too. He likes you, Pat. He likes you an awful lot. And I love you."

He did not answer.

"Do you hear me, Pat?"

Then suddenly it started to spill out of him. He told her the whole story about the past ten months. He left out nothing. He spared no details, nor did he spare himself. He told her everything. He took her hand and put it against his side where she could feel the bandage that covered the wound which was so well deserved. The wound from the bullet that should have killed. Finally he explained to her that if he made pictures of her father, or if he accepted Morris' offer, not only he but her father, would be ruined.

All she could say when he had finished was "Why? Why? Why?"

"Because your mother is mad," he said flatly. "Because she is old and sick of mind and afraid." Then he stood up and walked away from the table. She followed and trotted along beside him out of the bar and into the street and down the long blocks until they got to his apartment house.

Tony Ramova was sitting on the bench in the hall outside his door when he and Janey stepped out of the elevator. She was as beautiful as ever, but her eyes had a haunted look and her face bore the marks and ravages of fear and the deeply etched lines of excesses.

When Pat stepped out into the hall she rose and stood humbly by his door. She looked at Janey once, then paid no further attention to her. "May I come in and talk to you, Pat?" she asked.

"Go away," he said. "Go far, far away."

"Please," she said. "I've waited a long time."

He shrugged. "All right. Come on in. Why not?"

He opened the door and let Janey go in first, then waved Tony inside. He closed the door meticulously and went at once to the little cabinet. He extracted a bottle and asked, "Drink, anyone?"

Tony said, "Please." Janey said nothing, so he went to the kitchen and returned almost immediately with two glasses filled with ice cubes. He offered one to Tony and filled the glass from the bottle. Then he fixed himself one and said expansively, "Have a seat—anyplace."

He sat down himself on the floor, his back against the wall. Then he closed his eyes and seemed to pass out of the picture entirely. Janey went out into the kitchen. She put some water on the stove to boil for coffee and sat down at the kitchen table to wait out the session which was obviously coming.

In the studio Tony moved to stand in front of the disinterested Pat. She hesitated for a long time, then said, "Pat, I need you. Please come back to me."

"Yeah," he said.

"I mean it, Pat. I've learned an awful lesson."

"Lesson?" He did not open his eyes.

"Yes, Pat. I mean about your pictures. It was your pictures that made me. I know that now. It was your pictures, not myself."

"Are you slipping? Is that what you're trying to tell me?"

"Yes, I am. Oh, it's not that I'm out of business. It's nothing like that. It's just that the quality of the clubs that hire me isn't the same any more."

"You're just as good-looking as you ever were."

"That's not it, Pat. It's not my looks. It's *me* they don't like. They think I'm cheap or something. Those pictures made me look so good. Like I had class. You know what I mean?"

"Yeah, I know."

"So please, Pat, won't you come back?"

"What for?"

"To make some more pictures of me."

"You must have plenty of the old ones left."

"No. I've used them all trying to hang on to what I gained during your time. You destroyed all the negatives when you moved out. Please, Pat, I need you."

"After what you did to me?"

Her voice grew eager. "I'll make it up to you. You can have anything you want. Money. All the money you want. Me … *anything!*"

"No more of those damned parties?"

"No more. Honest, Pat."

For the first time he opened his eyes. "Go away," he said wearily.

"Please, Pat."

"I'm in enough trouble without adding you to it. Go away. I've had a bellyful of you. Or should I say a—*headful?*" he added wryly, rubbing the scar on his scalp.

"Gee, Pat," she said, kneeling. "I'm sorry about that. Honest. It was just that those awful pictures startled me so."

"I wouldn't be surprised," he said and closed his eyes again.

She stood up. "Look, Pat," she said. "Look, I'm still as good-looking as ever. Look."

He heard the rustle of her dress as she pulled it over her head. He opened his eyes a slit and watched disinterestedly as she stripped the slip from her figure. He closed them again and leaned his head back against the wall as she stood swaying before him, her beautiful body covered only by completely transparent white net panties.

"Look," she said. "Look, I didn't wear a brassiere. You always liked my breasts. You said so yourself." Her hands stroked over her breasts and they quivered a little under the touch. "Look," she pleaded, but he kept his eyes closed.

Suddenly she ripped the panties from her hips and stood naked before him. He might as well have been blind for all he saw. With his eyes closed, he lifted the drink to his lips and drained it. He called very loudly—more loudly than he needed. "Janey. Janey. Got that coffee ready?"

"You louse!" Tony sneered. "You dirty louse!"

"Amen," he muttered.

She went on, her voice hoarse with anger and terror. He could hear the sounds of her dressing under the snarl of her voice. "All right, Little Boy Blue. Suppose I set you straight, just for the record? It wasn't me that set you up with that studio. It wasn't me that paid you. It wasn't me that blackballed you in the business. It was Nell. *Nell,* do you hear? Every cent that was ever spent on you came from her. Do you really think I would go to such lengths to get a lousy photographer? I can get a dozen photographers any day of the week. And you can go to hell!"

The front door slammed as she left and he muttered softly to himself, "I probably will."

He heard the kitchen door open. Then Janey's voice came from across the room. "That was a cruel thing to do, Pat."

"I know," he said. "I know."

"Come and have some coffee."

He opened his eyes and the room seemed very bright to him after the darkness of his misery. "No, thanks. I want to go to bed. I want to sleep and sleep and sleep, and tomorrow I'll decide what has to be done. Right now I'm tired."

She came to him then and held him in her arms. "I'm tired, Janey," he repeated, like a little boy.

"I know, darling. Janey knows."

She helped him to his feet and half-carried him into his bedroom. She helped him undress, but the touch of her hands did nothing to him.

When he was asleep she sat beside his bed and looked at him. The tears were rolling down her cheeks.

CHAPTER ELEVEN

Pat opened his eyes to the morning sun that was streaming into the room. He rubbed his hands over his face and sat up. He looked around and was startled to find Janey asleep in the big chair by the window. Silently he got out of bed and put on a robe. He went out to the kitchen and put water on the stove for coffee. Then he went to the bathroom and took a quick shower. He shaved and dressed.

His mind was made up. He had three thousand dollars saved. There was only one thing he could do. He could leave Janey alone. He could leave the country and start over again someplace else. Someplace where Nell could not reach him. It was impossible for him to go on with Nell. But he could not break with her and stay in New York, or anywhere in the United States, for that matter. It was not only him now. It was Janey's father, too.

Pat's face twisted into a bitter grimace. Ten months ago it would never have occurred to him that any action of his would reflect on the life and fortune of one of the most successful and famous actors in the country.

When he was through dressing he pulled a suitcase from the top of the closet in the bedroom. Very quietly he opened drawers and cupboards and tossed the contents into the bag. When he was through he snapped it shut. He went to the kitchen and made himself a cup of scalding instant-coffee. When he had gulped it down, standing by the table, he put the water back on the stove to simmer. For Janey, he thought. Then he returned to the bedroom. He picked up the suitcase and got a topcoat from the closet.

Carrying his baggage, he stopped by Janey's chair. Goodbye, he thought. He bent down and started to kiss her, but thought the better of it.

He straightened up and left the room. On his way through the studio the phone rang. He considered letting it ring, but then realized it would wake Janey. He picked up the instrument.

It was Jacques Fribeaux. "What happened to you yesterday?"

Pat lied. "I forgot."

"That's a damned lie, and you know it," the accented voice taunted. "Those pictures were much too important to you for you to forget them."

Pat was speaking very softly, afraid he would wake Janey. "All right," he said, "so I didn't forget them."

"What happened?"

"I had a talk with Nell. That's what happened."

"I see. She talked you out of it?"

"You want to be ruined?"

"Let's put it this way: I'm already prepared to be ruined. Have you seen Janey?"

"Yes."

"Didn't she tell you?"

"Yes, she told me."

"So ... you see? I'm practically ruined anyway."

"Well, I'm not going to speed the matter. I've done enough already. Now if you'll excuse me, I was just on my way out."

"You're not running away, by any chance?"

"I had that in mind." He was about to hang up when he heard Janey's voice from behind him.

"Who's that?" she said.

He turned, holding the phone in his hand. She was standing in the door to the bedroom. She looked unbelievably beautiful.

Even in the morning, he thought irrelevantly. Even after a miserable night. "It's your father."

"Let me talk to him." She came forward eagerly, reaching for the instrument. He handed it over and she almost shouted into the mouthpiece. "Daddy! I want you to come over right away. Right away. I've got something very important to say to both you and Pat. All right? Right away." She hung up and then glanced at the bag and the coat. "Here, let me take those," she said and reached for them.

He handed them over as if he were in a daze and she put them on a chair by the front door. "If you still want them after I've had my say, they'll be right here," she said. "Now how about making me a cup of coffee while I fix my face?" She went to the bathroom and he returned sheepishly to the kitchen.

Like a small boy who has been naughty, he sat silently across the table from her while she drank the coffee. She seemed to be enjoying herself immensely. Her face sparkled and now and again she would glance at him out of the corner of her eye. Then a big smile would cover her face and a couple of times she chuckled out loud.

Pat's patience was almost at an end when the doorbell rang. He went to the front door and let Jacques Fribeaux into the studio. They went out to the kitchen where Janey was now pouring coffee for all of them.

"Sit down," she said. When they were sitting at the table, she placed the steaming cups before them. Then she sat down herself and looked from one to the other and smiled. "You two big dopes," she said. "You've been running and hiding from mother all this time, but I've thought of an answer to the whole mess."

Fribeaux leaned forward. "You've what?"

"Sure! It's so simple it's ridiculous!"

"I'll bet," said Pat, unconvinced.

"Look, what has mother bought with her ill-gotten gains? Respect. Position. Social prominence. Respectability. A virgin daughter on the market for a husband of good family and breeding. Park Avenue, in short. Now—what would intimidate mother more than anything else in the world?"

"You tell us. What?" said Fribeaux.

"Blackmail. That's what! A dose of her own medicine."

Pat stood up. "Oh now look, Janey, I've been all over that a thousand times. What do I have on your mother? Nothing. Oh, I've got plenty, all right, but nothing that I could ever prove in a court. If either your father or I tried to scare her with what we know, she would simply laugh at us."

"That's right, Janey," said Fribeaux.

Janey looked unbearably triumphant. "You've got her daughter! Her unsullied, untouched, socialite daughter, haven't you?"

Both men looked at her in complete incomprehension. "What are you getting at?" asked Pat.

"Oh, you *are* dopes," said Janey. Then she jumped to her feet and posed in the middle of the floor. She raised her skirt to her knees and cried, "So make some blackmail pictures of *me!*"

Pat stared at the girl in stunned amazement. It took a long time for the import of what she had suggested to sink in. When it did, he slammed his fist down on the table, making the coffee cups rattle in their saucers. "Are you crazy?" he shouted. "Are you out of your mind? Do you think for one minute I would do such a thing to you?"

Fribeaux said, "Just a second, Pat. Just a second. She's got something there."

Pat turned furiously on the older man. "You're her father!"

"So I am. So I am." The actor was quite complacent.

"Do you suggest that I do such a thing to your daughter?"

"Think about it for a minute, boy. Who's ever going to see those pictures? Janey's mother, who certainly is not going to show them to anybody, and you—well, how about you?"

"Yeah, how *about* me?"

Janey moved closer to Pat and asked in a very little voice, "Aren't you going to marry me?"

"Am I going to …? For heaven's sake, Janey, I'm in a thousand times worse position than I was the last time you brought this up."

Janey looked at her father with comic distress. "I'm always proposing to him, daddy, and he's always turning me down."

The actor shook his head. "Poor boy," he sighed exaggeratedly. "His head should perhaps be examined."

"This is not a joking matter," Pat said angrily. He left the kitchen abruptly and went into the large studio. He crossed the studio and entered the darkroom. When the door was closed and locked, he sat down on a stool in the darkness, his head in his hands.

The enormity of Janey's suggestion frightened him. He had done this to other women. He had hated it. He had loathed himself for doing it. He had fought against it. Could he do it to the woman he loved?

He looked back over the past ten months. How many innocent women had he helped blackmail? Was he innocent himself? Was he a victim as they had been victims? Would *they* look at it that way? How innocent *was* he?

He had three choices. He could leave the country and try to escape the whole mess. He could go to the police and ruin not only himself, but Janey's father, and he might get nothing for it except punishment for himself and not for Nell. He could take Janey's suggestion, and—maybe—live happily ever after. *Maybe.*

Suddenly he thought of the hobgoblin. Of the cheerful, kindly editor of *Skyline*—Bill Morris.

He reached out a hand and picked up the darkroom phone.

Yes, Mr. Morris was in his office. Yes, Mr. Morris would see him if he came over right away.

Pat went out to the kitchen and told the others what he was going to do. He explained carefully that the problem was more than he could handle. Janey and Fribeaux agreed to wait until he came back.

Morris stood up and greeted him enthusiastically when Pat entered his office.

"Boy," he cried. "Well, my boy. So you made up your mind, h'm?"

"No, sir, not quite yet."

"Huh? Not quite yet?" The editor sat down again. He looked doubtfully out of eyes that had a hard time remaining serious, even when confronted with Pat's troubled face. "What is it?" he asked in a surprisingly serious voice. "It doesn't take a mind-reader to see that you're in trouble."

Pat told him the whole story from beginning to end. Again, as he had been with Janey the night before, he was completely frank. He left out nothing, excused nothing.

When he was through, Morris sat quietly for a long time. "And what do you want from me, boy?" he asked finally.

"Advice, sir. That's all. I'm confused. I don't know which way to turn. I'm not able to measure the extent of my own guilt as far as the misfortunes of these women are concerned."

"They were blackmailed, weren't they?"

"Yes, sir."

"And what were you?"

"I?"

"What is blackmail?"

"Why, preying financially or materially on someone's fear, I suppose."

"So?"

"You mean that I was blackmailed, too?"

"Just as much as those women. You did what you did out of fear. Exactly the same kind of fear as theirs."

"That doesn't excuse me."

"No, it doesn't. But I would venture to say it is a mitigating circumstance."

"But what about Mr. Fribeaux?"

"Now, that's a little different. We don't know exactly what it is she has on him. He could perhaps be more seriously hurt than you."

"I just can't go straight to the police. It might ruin him."

Morris rose from his chair and came around to perch on the front of his desk. He was an entirely different Morris. A Morris that Pat would never have suspected existed under the cherubic exterior.

He said, "Look, boy, I tell you what. You've been honest with me. What's more—without knowing a damned thing about me, you have trusted me. You've come to me for help and I'm going to give it to you. I want you all in one piece, because I want you on my staff. No matter what happens to you during the next few months, I want you to know that your talent as a photographer is something I'm not going to sit around and watch the ruination of. Is that clear? All right, then. I'll tell you what to do. This is something we can't solve just like that. This will take a little time. I must have run twenty pictures in my magazine of the lady in question—at horse shows, at the opera, at the races and heaven knows where. And never—do you understand?—never have I heard one word against her. This will take a little sleuthing. So we need time. If your young lady is willing to do what she suggested, do it. Blackmail Mrs. Hamsun a little yourself. That will give us some time. Meanwhile I will get my noggin together with a couple of friends in the police department. If they can drum something up against her and you're willing to turn state's witness you may have to go up the river for a little while, but perhaps not for too long. And when you come back the young lady will be waiting, your job here with me will be waiting, and you'll have paid the price you have to pay for being a damned fool in the first place. Mr. Fribeaux we will make every effort to protect. How does that sound?"

When Pat left the office, Morris was already on the phone to police headquarters. The last the boy heard was the cheerful voice yelling as if the party on the end of the line was in the other room. "Hey, Ed, this is Morris. Now, damn it, you know who Morris is. I wish to hell I could pose for one of those pictures some time instead of just publishing them. Maybe some of my friends would recognize me then."

Pat made Jacques Fribeaux's pictures the following day. After the actor had left the studio Janey said, "Well, what are *we* waiting for?"

"Just stand there for a minute," Pat said. He adjusted the huge floods and sharp, cylindrical spotlights until the illumination seemed to form an aurora about her slender figure. He pulled a large velvet-covered couch from the wall and placed it directly behind her.

When he was through he said, "Do you really want to go through with this, Janey?"

"Watch me," she answered.

Her trim gabardine dress buttoned all the way down the front. Now she slowly undid the buttons, one by one. When the dress hung like a robe she shrugged out of it, her shoulders gleaming in the bright light. She pulled her slip over her head and stood before him in a white satin brassiere and outrageously scarlet panties.

She laughed when she saw the widening of his eyes. "Aren't they awful?" she asked. "I hate white panties. I always dye them some horrible color or other. I dyed these red when I was in college, but I never had the courage to wear them until I went looking for you yesterday."

She sat down on the edge of the bed and unsnapped her garters from the tops of the sheer stockings that covered her lovely, slim legs. Then she rolled the stockings off and pulled the garterbelt from her hips. She stood up again and reached behind her. With her eyes on his face she unhooked the strap behind her back and lifted the brassiere from her shoulders. She bent forward and slid the panties from her hips. Then she stood up straight. "Now what do I do?" she murmured.

"Wait a minute," he said softly. He went to the wall and flicked off all the lights but a lone little lamp that stood in a far corner. Then he came back to her. "The pictures can wait."

And then she was in his arms. "Be gentle," she whispered.

"I'll be gentle," he answered softly. His hands sought out her body and they sank back on the couch together. "I'll be so gentle ... always ... always and forever."

THE END

www.ingramcontent.com/pod-product-compliance
Lightning Source LLC
Chambersburg PA
CBHW052006240626
47153CB00008B/2764